A PLACE AMONG HEROES

HEROES

Book 1

Rise of Hope

The Liberty & Property Legends in reading order:

HEARTLAND
On the Side of Angels

EMPIRE FOR LIBERTY
Dangerous Lullaby

FIRST COUNTRY
Tinged with Rose

THE HOUR OF EVIDENCE
Deceived

A PLACE AMONG HEROES
Book 1: *Rise of Hope*

A PLACE AMONG HEROES

HEROES

Book 1

Rise of Hope

TERRI SEDMAK

THE
LIBERTY & PROPERTY
LEGENDS

This novel is a work of fiction.

Visit www.terrisedmak.com
Official website of THE LIBERTY & PROPERTY LEGENDS
A Saga of The West & Gilded Age

Heartfelt thanks to my enthusiastic team of beta-readers;
your expertise and attention to detail are very much appreciated.

Literary credits: *We Will Not Be Slaves*, Sons of Liberty Traditional; *Emma* by
Jane Austen; *Something Left Undone* and *The Rainy Day* by Henry Wadsworth
Longfellow; *Lorica of St Patrick (St Patrick's Breastplate)*, also known as *The Cry of
the Deer* by St Patrick of Ireland, 433 A.D. Scripture taken from the Holy Bible,
New International Version; Copyright 1973, 1978,1984 International Bible
Society; used by permission of Zondervan Bible Publishers.

Cover and seal graphics: Blow–Up Design Pty Ltd

THE LIBERTY & PROPERTY LEGENDS™
Tank & Ferry Entertainment
Sydney, Australia

Published by VIVID Publishing
P.O. Box 948, Fremantle
Western Australia, 6959
www.vividpublishing.com.au

National Library of Australia Cataloguing-in-Publication entry:
Sedmak, Terri
A place among heroes : book 1 rise of hope
ISBN: 978-1-925681-83-3 (paperback)
Series: The Liberty & Property Legends
A823.4

For Matt

'The birthright we hold, shall never be sold,
but sacred maintained to our graves,
and before we'll comply, we'll gallantly die,
for we must not, we will not be slaves, brave boys,
for we must not, we will not be slaves.'

The Sons of Liberty

Happiness is like a butterfly; the more you chase it, the more
it will elude you, but if you turn your attention to other things,
it will come and sit softly on your shoulder.

Henry David Thoreau

Every moment of light and dark is a miracle.

Walt Whitman

These are the days that must happen to you.

Walt Whitman

All streams flow into sea, but the sea is never full.
To the place where the streams come from,
there they return again.

Book of Ecclesiasticus

Tressa...

"Admit you are trapped."

My reflection in the armoire mirror admits it.

Whatever Mart's expectations had been for me, he could not have foreseen the direction my life has taken. How could anyone? Although I should have. The impulse to join my life to Mart's had been too urgent to ignore, of the kind that a wise person knows to examine carefully. But I am not a wise person. I don't know how to be, even after everything that has happened. And hindsight doesn't count. Neither am I brave. An act of desperation is not bravery.

If I were to take up my watercolors and paint myself, there would exist a portrait of a pale woman clinging to a twine bridge that is suspended over a gray abyss; one move in any direction and I could lose my footing and be falling. In some ways I am already falling. So I grasp tighter to what I have.

Exactly what makes me cling to hope and not fall into utter despair I don't know. Who fully comprehends the whole notion of hope anyhow? Certainly, I have the right to pursue happiness and freedom which dignifies every human being by right of birth, and I have yet to entertain in any serious way the idea that these things might not come to me and underpin my life and make it authentic, although it has crossed my mind; some would say I have everything one could possibly need, and yet I don't have these. Because my life isn't my own. Trapped...

I live by gratitude; I practice deep and abiding loyalty. Always. So, for now, while everything stays as it is, while everyone lives on this knife's edge, that twine bridge remains tightly in my grasp; and hope for my life seems as viable as it does for all of them.

ONE

Labour with what zeal we will,
Something still remains undone,
Something uncompleted still
Waits the rising of the sun.

Till at length the burden seems
Greater than our strength can bear,
Heavy as the weight of dreams,
Pressing on us everywhere.

Henry Wadsworth Longfellow
Something Left Undone

Andy Marks

Cheyenne, Friday
Twelfth day into the Trial
Day Nine of Testimony

"How was the train?"

"How do you think?"

"You look fine to me, Mead. Couldn't have been that bad."

"Slept all night in third class have you, Buchanan?"

"Hell, no…"

"Course not. So. You want this information on Lamont or not?"

"That's what you are being paid for, Mead, unless of course what you have is disappointing."

"I never disappoint, Buchanan. You know that."

"Let's not stand here on the platform all day… that's your entire luggage?"

"I don't intend to stay long. Let's hurry it up. It's cold and I need a drink."

"It's nine o'clock in the morning, for God's sake."

"So?"

"Court starts at eleven. Morning session has been delayed an hour due to a fire in the courthouse. We've plenty of time to review what you have…"

"A fire?"

"Yet another delay. The Judge granted Faraday an extra day's recess to allow the sheriff to return from Bright River after fetching the deed to the Diamond-T.

"Whatever, Buchanan. Your problems don't interest me…"

After waiting for them to move away, Andy steps out from inside the luggage room onto the platform. He watches Buchanan march off, still talking fast and loose with an ill-mannered, sour-faced man who in another outfit could pass for a bounty hunter. But in that get up, rumpled clothes and unshaven face, he looks like a malcontented, underpaid spy.

"Careless, Buchanan," Andy murmurs to himself.

❖

"What do you mean you followed Buchanan down to the depot this morning?"

"I'm looking out for my client, Ryan. I told you that."

Sheriff Ryan rubs his forehead above one eye. He looks tired, maybe even exhausted. "Your client is fine..." He throws out his hand in the direction of the interrogation room next door to his office; through the glass pane in the door Andy espies the top of Lamont's head as he sits chained to the desk, leisurely reading the morning papers.

Ryan sighs and says, "All right, Marks. What did you hear?"

"Buchanan hired someone by the name of Mead to investigate Lamont. He met this Mead at the train and they went off together so Mead could divulge the contents of his discovery."

Ryan frowns. "Mead?"

"Sour-faced character."

"So? Buchanan's been up to a little investigation of his own."

"I want assurances from you that Lamont is not in any danger."

Ryan smirks. "Take a look at him, Marks. He looks better than you or me."

"Definitely better than you. Are you sure you are up to the task of protecting my client?"

"What do you think? In case you hadn't heard, counselor, we had a fire in the courthouse this morning; the prisoner holding room and the transfer corridor to the jail. Pioneer Hook and Ladder got onto it but the damage is done, we can't use it. So some of us have had a long morning."

"I heard. Everyone has, Ryan. News spread like wildfire, if you'll pardon the pun. Word on the street is all prisoners are likely to be transferred via the side entrance by your office. You got yourself a good old-fashioned pretty pickle."

"And you to tell me these things," Ryan fires back. He frowns thoughtfully. "Something else on your mind?"

"You shouldn't have exposed Lamont."

"Maybe. It doesn't matter now. This morning Lamont will be on the stand and giving testimony. What Buchanan knows or doesn't know won't change what Lamont is about to reveal about Bodecker."

"Mead might know things that will discredit Lamont."

"Cam will defuse Lamont's vices. Listen, Marks, is there something you want to tell me about Lamont?"

"Lamont is my first big client in this town. If anything goes wrong he will probably be my last."

Ryan folds his arms and says dismissively, "See you in court."

As Andy turns to leave, Ryan adds, "Oh, what train did this Mead get off – Denver?"

Andy gives a curt nod. "I don't like this, Ryan. Just so you know."

Ryan acknowledges him with a meager chin toss.

"Lamont might know of this Mead," Andy says.

"Either way it might change his outlook. You can't say anything, Marks."

Andy clenches his jaw. "This had better not go up in smoke, Ryan."

"And just so *you* know, Marks, the pun is sadly overrated."

Josh

Swathes of black staining the walls and ceiling. Smoke hovering over puddles of hot ash. That godawful smell…

Standing back from the doorway with Cam, surveying the fire damage to the room and the corridor beyond, Josh pushes up his spectacles and imagines the flames devouring the room and rapidly spreading into the corridor; he's trying to ignore the acrid smell ripping into his nostrils, the smoke that's stinging his eyes, and the headache that's being exacerbated by Pioneer Hook and Ladder as some of the men shore up the ceiling by hammering long beams into place, while others putter about in the debris.

He doesn't usually have the imagination for such things; perhaps something of Emmaline Roberts has rubbed off on him since her turn of phrase afforded the reader a strong vision of most everything she wrote about. And perhaps it is the sickening thought of the trial being delayed till the damage can be repaired that's filling his empty stomach with a sense of defeat. He could use some breakfast. They all could. Worst morning he can remember.

They were all so grateful the jail wasn't affected. The prisoners had been removed to the yard in the darkness and heavily guarded while the fire was extinguished. The tension that gripped him until the moment they were safely returned to their cells (complaining about the smell and residual smoke), caused his headache. The whole episode was one big headache for everyone.

Judge Callaghan's clerk appears out of the corner of his eye.

Cam sees him, too. "What is it, McArdle?"

"The Judge wants everyone in his chambers – now."

Cam gives him a polite nod. "We could all use some food. Would you mind seeing to it?"

"Getting you your breakfast is not my job, Mr Faraday. I reckon that's what Mrs Faraday's for. But as luck would have it, there's no need to worry." McArdle shrugs as though being rude and casual toward his superior and a man as important as Cam is something he cares little about. "It's already there. Baskets of food. Martha sent them over. Coffee, flapjacks, biscuits, eggs, steaks for Cliff… speak of the devil, I need to go find him and Mac…"

Two-faced, nasty little prick.

"Then let's give three cheers for Martha and none for you," Cam mutters after McArdle has done them both a favor and left.

And yet Josh feels hope rising from the ashes – even if Jeff McArdle is the worst clerk ever, and didn't deserve to work for the Judge and everyone thought so.

It's good to be appreciated.

Faraday

Cheyenne Courthouse
Two hours later
Lamont has been sworn in

"You may proceed, Mr Faraday."

"Thank you, Your Honor. Mr Lamont, would you please state your full name, current address and occupation for the court."

"Christopher Peter Lamont. I live in Capitol Hill, Denver, Colorado. I'm a businessman."

"Thank you, Mr Lamont, now if…"

"Objection, Your Honor. The witness's occupation is vague. I'm sure the court would like to know what kind of businessman?"

"Your Honor, we have barely begun…"

"Overruled, Mr Buchanan. The witness's occupation will stay. Let Mr Faraday present his case and the witness his testimony."

"Your Honor, I believe that the witness's occupation has a bearing on the defense of my client…"

"There is such a thing as cross-examination, Mr Buchanan, which, I might add, you have had no problem employing to this point." Judge Callaghan's jaunty delivery appears to stop Buchanan in his tracks and he resumes his seat. "Proceed, Mr Faraday."

"Thank you, Your Honor." Faraday slides his hands in his pockets. "Mr Lamont, you are currently serving a one month sentence for assault in the fifth degree on a saloon girl in town, is that correct?"

The jury seems to suck in its breath as one, counterpoint to the puckered murmuring from the gallery. Meanwhile, Mead the sour-faced informant Cliff warned him about sits in the front row wearing a gleeful smirk. There's something grubby about that man.

"That's so."

"Why did you do this, Mr Lamont?"

"Because I was missing the woman I love."

"She is very special to you?"

"Yes, Mr Faraday. The only woman in the world for me."

"And you couldn't be with her?"

"No. I tried to pretend with the girl in the saloon. She didn't like it and reported me to the sheriff. I got a month in the territorial penitentiary. I'm very sorry she got hurt..."

"Objection. All very touching, Your Honor, but where is the relevance of this criminal's testimony to my client?"

"Mr Lamont is not a criminal, Your Honor. He made a mistake under emotional distress."

The Judge's bottom jaw moves from side to side as though he has something indigestible in his mouth. "Overruled, Mr Buchanan. I think we should see where Mr Faraday is leading us."

Buchanan sits.

"Now, Mr Lamont, who is the woman you miss so greatly?"

"Eva Tarrant."

Louder murmurs circulate the courtroom. The Judge lightly taps his gavel.

"Is it true that Eva Tarrant is Loren Bodecker's mistress?"

"She used to be."

"Used to be?"

"She moved on to someone else, before me that is."

"Who was that?"

"Dillon Kerr."

The courtroom erupts outright.

"Order, order... order!"

"And you know Dillon Kerr?"

"Sure I know him. He works for me."

Rumblings break out again.

"But everyone here in this courtroom knows that Dillon Kerr is the defendant Loren Bodecker's Cheyenne attorney. How is it that Dillon Kerr works for you?"

"That gets complicated. You see, Dillon was only pretending to work for Bodecker. I set him up here in Cheyenne as my spy."

While the Judge deals with the outbreak of unrest, Faraday slips a glance at Loren Bodecker. A white bed sheet flapping on a clothesline displays more color. When all is quiet again, Faraday continues…

"Who else knows about this, Mr Lamont?"

"Apart from yourself and Mr Ryan, no one."

"Not even Mr Bodecker?"

"Hec, no, look at him. He's turned white as a ghost…"

The gallery chortles and again the Judge gavels for quiet.

"Mr Lamont, what was the purpose of having Dillon Kerr pose as Mr Bodecker's attorney to spy on him?"

"Well, Mr Bodecker owns… *owned* a big empire. Silver mines, coal mines, a cattle kingdom, just to name a few. His empire stretches clean across the country, even got European investors. I wanted Dillon to keep an eye on Bodecker's activities."

"Because Mr Bodecker is your rival?"

"Not exactly. You see, Mr Bodecker's empire wasn't his to begin with. It was mine. In fact, he took it off me, and it rightfully belongs to me."

While Buchanan stands to object, the courtroom's barely held composure collapses into disarray. Above it Buchanan's strident voice can be heard…

"This man is a convicted rapist and woman basher, who can believe him? No one! No one can believe him!"

The entire cohort of the jury appears to have reached the limits of its capability to fathom, either collectively or as individuals; its members are demonstrably astonished by what is transpiring before their eyes and ears.

Judge Callaghan tenaciously regains control of his courtroom. "I will clear the court if I hear so much as a whisper. A whisper I tell you! If I see so much as a *look* between two people! I hope I have made myself clear."

In quick order, one could hear a pin drop.

"Mr Lamont," Faraday continues, "how did Loren Bodecker take your empire off you?"

"He got himself onto the boards of my companies; with money or by other means, he bought off all my shareholders and had me kicked out. Over time he became the majority shareholder of half my companies. The other half of my empire I managed to sure up before he got to them. Meanwhile he decided to bully other owners out of their companies, using the same methods, manipulating and buying off shareholders and board members and managers. He gets a hold on people so that in the end he owns them. Latest example would be Richard Taylor's sand and gravel mining company. That concern was traveling well enough the way it was, but Richard Taylor is an ambitious man, like Bodecker is, so when Bodecker offered him a way into coal mining here in Wyoming, Taylor couldn't say no to letting Bodecker onto the board…"

"Objection. Your Honor, I fail to see how the witness's knowledge about Richard Taylor's business affairs is admissible. At the very least he's read it in the papers, at best it is hearsay, courtesy of his so-called spy!"

The Judge looks thoughtful. "Mr Faraday, what say you?"

"Your Honor, if the witness could be allowed to finish I'm sure Mr Buchanan will be relieved of his objections."

"You may continue with the witness… Overruled."

Buchanan sits, miffed.

"Mr Lamont," Faraday continues, "you were saying that Richard Taylor couldn't say no to admitting Mr Bodecker to the board of his mining company. How *do* you know about Richard Taylor, Mr Lamont?"

"I already told you that I had a spy. Dillon Kerr knew all about Mr Bodecker's activities…"

"Objection! Your Honor, as I suspected this is all hearsay and…"

"Your Honor, Mr Kerr was employed by Mr Lamont to obtain information relevant to his ongoing battle with Mr Bodecker. What Mr Lamont knows about the defendants and their activities is not something he picked up on a street corner or told to him by some disgruntled employee. Mr Kerr was hired for the specific purpose of obtaining information. What he communicated to Mr Lamont cannot be considered hearsay."

"Your Honor, this is preposterous."

"Mr Faraday," the Judge says, frowning.

"Your Honor," Faraday continues, crossing to his table and receiving a pocket-sized journal with a blue cover from Josh's outstretched hand. "I wish to enter into evidence People's exhibit 16: Dillon Kerr's journal..." He holds it up for the jury to see. "In it he has logged times and dates of his covert activities as well as the dates on which he sent reports to Mr Lamont. It was given to Sheriff Ryan by Dillon Kerr himself on the night Kerr sold out Mr Lamont to Mr Ryan for the woman Eva Tarrant..."

The courtroom erupts into chaos again. The gavel resounds so forcefully Faraday is aware of his eardrums vibrating.

"The court thanks counsel for the evidence. Mr Buchanan, your objection is overruled," the Judge says firmly. "Mr Faraday, please continue."

"Where did you keep the written reports Mr Kerr sent you, Mr Lamont?"

"They were kept in my safe at my home in Denver, but..."

Again, Josh hands him the evidence. He approaches Lamont and passes him the portfolio. "Look at this portfolio, if you will, Mr Lamont, and then tell the court what you see."

"These are the reports and such that Dillon Kerr sent me on Mr Bodecker and Mr Donnelly. Yes... this is them. See, that's where I sign and date as they come in. I keep good records..."

"Your Honor, if it pleases the court, exhibit 17: the dossier containing dozens of written reports and telegrams composed and sent by Dillon Kerr to Mr Lamont in the course of his work as Mr Lamont's spy. Mr Lamont gave the prosecution access to his safe, and United States Marshal Dan Hummer procured the evidence and brought it to Cheyenne. The marshal arrived last night and many hours were spent verifying the contents."

Faraday glances at the back of the courtroom. Dan Hummer stands by the doors, arms folded across a puffed up chest, his big, usually animated face inscrutable for once.

"Objection, Your Honor, this is... this is...."

The Judge sends Buchanan a hard look over his spectacles. "It is called doing your homework, Mr Buchanan. Overruled."

14

"Your Honor…"

"Overruled, Mr Buchanan."

Next, Faraday retrieves the dossier from Lamont and finds the page he wants. "Mr Lamont, would you read the lines that are underlined on that page?"

"Loren will infiltrate Taylor Mining using the same method he always does, via the board. Once he has control of it, he will use it as a pawn in the war with the Alliance."

Lamont closes it politely and hands it over.

Faraday holds on to it. He is not finished with him.

"Mr Lamont, did you know of Mr Bodecker and Mr Donnelly's plot to destroy the Alliance?"

Lamont clears his throat. "Yes."

Murmurs swirl around the courtroom like wind.

"Did you know of Ed Parsons' involvement with Mr Bodecker and Mr Donnelly?"

"Yes."

"Why then didn't you come forward at the Parsons trial?"

"Because Loren Bodecker warned me that if I did I would be killed on sight. Donnelly's mavericks, Mr Faraday. Murdered the Keaton girl in cold blood. The mavericks were a formidable deterrent and weapon. That they have been wiped from the face of the earth is a mercy, and a credit to those involved."

"Quite so. But what use was the espionage if you were too intimidated or uncomfortable to use it, Mr Lamont?"

"Well, you see, I knew there would come a day when all things being equal I would have a chance. That chance came when Mr Ryan went up to Donnelly's ranch outside Laramie to find Dillon Kerr. He didn't know Dillon wasn't crooked, and only a spy. But Dillon told him about me so he'd have a chance with Eva. Then, when I realized I could trust that you and Mr Ryan were genuine in prosecuting Bodecker and Donnelly for murder and conspiracy, and that you wouldn't give up no matter what the threats or the outcome or personal cost to yourselves or the sacrifices you were prepared to make, I knew this was my chance."

"Did you know that the maverick was going to kill Miss Keaton?"

"No, no, that I didn't know until Dillon sent me a report. He didn't know it was going to happen either. In his report he said he thought Bodecker and Donnelly kept that entirely to themselves…"

Now Sturrock is on his feet. "Objection…"

"One minute, Your Honor…." Faraday thumbs through the dossier and finds the relevant page. "Read this if you would, Mr Lamont…"

Lamont squints and reads. *"Just when I thought it was all over Donnelly sends a maverick to kill the Keaton girl. A barbaric and senseless act. And one which the Alliance will feel for the rest of its days. If you were to ask me why he did it I would have to say that Bodecker wanted Luke Taylor on his knees and the whole Alliance brought down after their victory over Parsons. Capitulation, discharged in its most evil form, is his one goal."*

Behind him, Faraday hears heart-wrenching sobs coming from the gallery.

"Objection overruled," the Judge murmurs. Sturrock resumes his seat.

"Mr Lamont, how did you respond to this report?" Faraday asks.

"I was downright shocked, but it only served to remind me of what Donnelly and Bodecker were capable and I had to be very careful. After all, I had spread the word to anyone who would listen how Bodecker operated. I was his corporate enemy and therefore I had become his mortal enemy."

"As the defendants began to mount the attack against the Alliance, Dillon Kerr continued to send you reports?"

"Yes, but they became less frequent. I suspect now that Dillon had taken on Eva Tarrant as his mistress since Bodecker had left town for Omaha and left Eva behind. When Luke Taylor left Cheyenne and went to San Francisco after the Keaton girl was murdered, Donnelly and Bodecker began to plan a very calculated attack on the Alliance… it's all in the file there… I don't think anyone expected Taylor to return though. He's been a thorn in the side of the Empire for a long time."

"Mr Lamont, why were you, a prominent businessman, employed at the Cheyenne Club as a desk clerk?"

Lamont looks at the jury and says, "Actually, I wasn't. The day Mr Ryan, Ben Taylor and young Raina Montgomery came to rescue Richard Taylor that was the only time I've been the desk clerk. I had discovered Bodecker was holding Richard Taylor there. I sneaked inside several times to check on him. I think Taylor probably thinks of me as his keeper, but in fact I was keeping him alive. Bodecker hardly cared about him, and he had been using him as a puppet all over town to do his bidding, blackmailing him that if he didn't do as he was told, Bodecker would kill his wife and son. The poor feller was so sick and disoriented by the time Mr Ryan came along... Anyhow, that particular day I was planning to get Taylor out of the Club myself and take him away to some place safe and let him go. I had a whole plan worked out and being the desk clerk was part of it. Anyway, Mr Ryan and the others came along so I backed off my plan and left the lawman and Taylor's son Ben to do their job."

"Why did you feign at first that Richard Taylor wasn't there, and they couldn't see him in the end?"

"What Raina and Ben Taylor didn't know was that the desk clerk who I was filling in for had returned and was putting on his coat in the back office. He could hear everything. If I had told them where Taylor was, Bodecker would have come after me. I went along with what they were doing, pretending to let them distract me so that Ben Taylor could follow Mr Ryan inside the Club to look for Ben's father. It was something at least. Then I hung about making sure the desk clerk was busy." Lamont looks across the courtroom at Cliff and says, "Sorry if it lessens your achievements, Sheriff."

Faraday can't imagine anyone would think so; nevertheless warm-hearted chuckles arise from the gallery of onlookers.

Cliff looks as though he didn't even hear him. And much too focused to let any attempt at humor distract him.

"Mr Lamont, why didn't Mr Bodecker just kill you and be done with it?"

"He tried in the beginning. He sent assassins. Arranged accidents. But I got smart and I fought back. And I protected myself. And with Dillon as my spy in Cheyenne I could keep track of things up here."

"Mr Lamont, you sent Dillon Kerr a telegram about the same time that Loren Bodecker was arrested."

Ever-prepared, Josh hands Faraday the relevant telegram.

"Read this, please, Mr Lamont."

"LOREN COMPROMISED. YOU KNOW WHAT YOU HAVE TO DO."

"What does that mean, Mr Lamont?"

"Dillon's a spy. Not a killer. To hear Mr Ryan tell it, he was a pain in the a… a right pain around town, but he was only doing his job. I know he has his odd points, kinda highbrow an' all, but I didn't want him getting arrested and dragged into the mess, complicating things. That's why he fled up to the ranch. Donnelly wasn't going to be using it so we agreed to meet there and stay there secretly while the trial was going on. A body could move around now the mavericks were gone. Dillon and I made a deal to stand by each other."

"Your Honor, People's exhibit 18: the telegram sent to Dillon Kerr by the witness Mr Lamont on learning of the defendant's impending trouble with the Law." Faraday places the telegram on the evidence table.

"Thank you, Mr Faraday. Continue."

"Now, Mr Lamont, could you please tell the court who your grandfather was."

"My grandfather was…"

"Objection. Really, Your Honor, I fail to see the relevance of Mr Lamont's family tree."

"Your Honor, my learned colleague fails because he lacks patience…"

"That will do, Mr Faraday. Mr Buchanan, I believe I must overrule you once more."

Buchanan takes his seat once more. Beside him, Bodecker sits expressionless and pasty. Behind *him*, the informant Mead wears a scowling expression. Faraday takes a walk towards the jury panel, whose members sit up a little, as he intended.

"Your grandfather, Mr Lamont."

"My grandfather, Mr Faraday, was Archie Connors."

Luke

Luke tightens his arm around Sara's shoulders in the hope that more support will deliver some comfort; her weeping is sometimes the only sound in the room apart from Cam's voice or Lamont's. Her open grief disquiets him, creates a ball of fear in his gut. Sure, the truth is finally coming out, but how does he help his mother who is nowhere near as battle-hardened as the rest of them? He fears she will sink into despair and never recover.

"And who is Archie Connors?" Cam asks.

"Archie Connors is the man from whom Luke Taylor's father, Morgan, and Ethan Benchley, his partner, bought the land now known as the Diamond-T."

"So your grandfather Archie Connors owned the land now called the Diamond-T and sold it to Morgan Taylor and Ethan Benchley."

"That's correct."

"Mr Lamont, your grandfather Archie Connors became a wealthy man, correct?"

"Yes."

"And on his death he left the bulk of his estate to you?"

"Yes."

"And you used that considerable inheritance to build up your business empire?"

"Yes."

"And not only did you inherit his monetary wealth, but also a number of properties. In fact, you hold the deeds to no less than ten sizeable parcels of real estate in California alone."

"Yes."

"When did you come into your inheritance, Mr Lamont?"

"My grandfather died ten years ago."

"And your parents never inherited?"

"No, my parents died twelve years ago, two years before my grandfather, so they never inherited. Grandpa changed his will."

"How did your grandfather obtain his wealth?"

A smile forms on Lamont's face. "He was a gold prospector."

"He went about the country looking for gold. And obviously found a great deal of it?"

"Yes, he followed all the gold rushes; and silver and gems."

"In fact, your grandfather even went abroad in search of gold."

"Yes, he even went to Australia."

"And where is Australia?"

"Australia is a British colony in the Southern Hemisphere. To hear my grandfather tell it, he said people from all over the world had gone to the goldfields there, places called Bendigo and Ballarat. He came home and started to consolidate; he invested, bought real estate and such."

"Real estate that included the ranch now called The Diamond-T, which he sold to Morgan Taylor and Ethan Benchley."

"Yes."

Sara has decided to stop crying, and now sits a stiff as a marble statue, listening as if her life depended upon it.

Luke removes his arm, glances at Jennifer on the other side of him and meets her intense green eyes. She takes his hand and enfolds it within both of hers, her cool, calm touch soothing the uncomfortable knot in his stomach.

"Was the sale straight forward?" Cam is asking meanwhile.

"Not exactly."

"How so?"

"Back in those days my grandfather was determined to be a successful prospector. He started out as a land speculator on the frontier and did all right. His real estate portfolio grew hand in hand with his gold prospecting. In the territories, the Army hadn't yet eradicated the land of Indians, or got 'em all on reserves. When Morgan Taylor came along from Texas, looking for new pastures here in the north, he found that my grandfather had some grazing land to sell. Grandpa'd had the Army survey it so the railroads and the prospectors couldn't get their hands on it. But the survey revealed something curious. A reef of quartz ore."

All around him Luke is aware of growing whispers.

Lamont, deep into his story, continues. "When they got together to negotiate, my grandfather had a proposition for Morgan. Grandpa would sell Morgan all the land except for a three mile stretch from a place later called Diamond Pass through the valley up to the Plateau. This Grandpa would lease to Morgan for grazing cattle while he was gone."

"Gone, Mr Lamont?"

Lamont blinks. "Grandpa went off to make more money aiming to return and take back the three mile stretch when things got more civilized. The Frontier was a violent place after the war."

Whispers escalate to loud murmurs.

The Judge bangs his gavel.

Cam pushes on. "So, what you are saying, Mr Lamont, is that Ethan Benchley, Luke Taylor and Sara Taylor do not own the three mile stretch of the Diamond-T, but you do because it is part of your inheritance from your grandfather?"

"That's correct."

Luke feels sick. Jennifer's fingers tighten their grip on his hand. On his right he feels Sara's trembling hand slide beneath his arm, her fingers wrapping around his sleeve.

The Judge is forced to call order yet again.

At the prosecution's table, Josh hands Cam a familiar-looking document, and one other.

"Mr Lamont, I have here the deed to the Diamond-T, also known as the Connors Bill of Sale. I would ask you to read the condition of ownership in the second paragraph please."

Lamont takes the document, swallowing like he had a brick lodged in the back of his throat. *"It is agreed upon that the parcel of land, to wit the three square miles from the high pass in the south to the plateau boundary in the north and including the valley in between, shall never be used for any other purpose than grazing cattle, nor shall it be fenced or closed up for any reason, nor will it be sold to another party."*

"To your knowledge, Mr Lamont, what was the intention behind this condition?"

"Grandpa intended to return with mining equipment and an engineer to survey the three mile stretch, Mr Faraday, for *gold*."

At that moment, with *that* word, the tenuous order demanded by the Judge collapses and the room is in utter chaos; meanwhile Cam continues loud and hard, "Located within the quartz ore…"

"Yes, that's correct," Lamont strains above Judge Callaghan hammering his bench. The Judge may as well be hammering the air.

All about them, from jury panel to public gallery, the prospect of gold obliterates the composure of every person in the room. All, that is, but the Alliance. Every one of them is frozen to their seat as the cold truth dribbles like icy water over their heads and down their bodies; unable to utter a word or even breathe; shunted into a vacuum of disbelief.

Luke forces himself out of it.

Men are on their feet shouting at one another, shouting at Lamont, at Bodecker and Donnelly. Luke's chest rumbles with the thunder of their protest. Sara covers her ears. It's madness.

"Order! Order! I will have order in this courtroom!"

Cliff moves quickly around the room, confronting several of the men with a different prospect. Contempt of court. Several back down, resume their seats, and the rest follow.

Cam waits for several long moments of persistent quiet before he continues. "When did you learn of the deed to the Diamond-T, Mr Lamont?"

Lamont, shaken and needing to clear his throat more than once, adds another long pause in the proceedings before he answers. "My grandfather's copy of the Bill of Sale was always kept with his other official papers and documents in the vault in the Bank of California in San Francisco. Three years ago I decided to go through these papers again and see what was there, perhaps sell some property. And I discovered the Bill of Sale with its unusual clause."

"Mr Lamont, how do you know all these details about the Diamond-T and your grandfather and the agreement he had with Morgan Taylor? – because the clause refers only to the conditions for use of the land."

"Yes, I understand. Uh… you see, in the safety deposit box with the Bill of Sale was a journal. It was all written down, everything I'm telling you. And it contained my grandfather's signature and that of….of…"

Don't say it, don't say his name.

"Morgan Taylor."

That rumbling in Luke's chest explodes.

Who is *this* Morgan Taylor?

Who in God's name is his father?

Breaking contact with both Jennifer and his mother, he shoots to his feet. "No, I don't believe it. I don't believe it!"

He hears Sara's muffled cry.

Everyone turns their eyes upon him.

He glares at Lamont.

Lamont looks pityingly at him. "It's all there, Taylor. I'm sorry, but it's the truth."

The Judge says, "Resume your seat, Mr Taylor."

"It's not…" he rasps, choking on a gulp of emotion, "true."

"The truth will set you free," Lamont replies, "cold and hard though it may be."

The truth isn't cold. Oh, no. It's a fire, consuming the comfortable lies, and laying bare the easy virtue of silence.

"Your Honor," Cam says, "if I may suggest a ten minute recess."

Recess… *Now?*

But the Judge is agreeing. The crisp crack of his gavel makes it official.

The Judge leaves and the entire room breaks into a mad scramble.

Jennifer is standing by his side, looking up at him.

"It's all right, Luke," she whispers and her hand slips into his, grasping it firmly. "Everything will be all right. Let's get some fresh air."

Faraday

Session resumes

"Your Honor, if it pleases the court, this is People's exhibit 19: Archie Connors' copy of the deed to the Diamond-T, also known as the Connors Bill of Sale; and this, People's exhibit 20: the journal which documents the circumstances of the secret agreement between Connors and Morgan Taylor."

"Thank you, Mr Faraday. You may continue with the witness."

"Thank you, Your Honor. Mr Lamont, why didn't you call in the agreement made between your grandfather and Morgan Taylor with the present owners of the Diamond-T?"

"Well, you see it's like this. At the same time I was sorting through all the legal ramifications and looking into the kind of people the Taylors and Benchleys were, and if they would fight me in court for the three mile stretch, I discovered I had an unexpected rival for the quartz ore."

"I see. And who would that be?"

"Ed Parsons, owner of the land to the north of the Diamond-T."

"He had discovered the quartz ore?"

"Yes. And from my understanding he knew about it for some time. He was determined to get the Taylors off their land so he could get access to the ore. I had some of his activities in the courts investigated. He challenged Luke Taylor in court regarding the Bill of Sale at least half a dozen times in three years. The unusual clause must have tipped him off. But how he found out about the clause in the first place, I don't know."

"I can answer that, Mr Lamont," Faraday says, sliding his hands in his pockets and smiling at the jury, "it was common knowledge. The story of how the Taylors and the Benchleys came to Wyoming and settled in the Bright River district is family history and local history. Now, what were you doing while Ed Parsons was attempting to take over the Diamond-T?"

"I would have told Parsons to back off and take his greedy hands elsewhere except I found out that his financial backer and partner was Loren Bodecker, my enemy."

"Why didn't you go to the authorities?"

"Well, you see, if Bodecker had found out who owned the three mile stretch he would've killed me. The courts couldn't have protected me; he'd have killed me for the deed…"

"Objection, Your Honor. The witness is speculating. There is no proof of this."

"Merely Mr Bodecker's previous dealings with Mr Lamont," Faraday refutes.

The Judge looks at jury. "Still, such a statement is to be disregarded. Objection sustained."

Faraday is not prepared to let the matter go. "So you feared for your life if Mr Bodecker found out you owned the three mile stretch?"

"Precisely," Lamont says agreeably.

"Your silence cost the lives of John and Amy Keaton's children, Mr Lamont," Faraday says. "The Keatons allied themselves with the Taylors and the Benchleys against Ed Parsons because they thought he wanted their grazing lands and their water."

"I was sorry to hear about that. But my hands were tied. I was caught between a rock and a hard place."

"Mr Lamont, why did your grandfather never return to the Diamond-T and the three mile stretch?"

Lamont frowns. "He became wealthy. Rich. In all my life he never mentioned the land in Wyoming once to me. I think he forgot about it."

"That seems somewhat unlikely, Mr Lamont."

"Might seem that way, but you didn't know my grandfather."

Faraday strides across to the evidence table and takes up

Archie Connors' journal. He finds the place he wants and walks it back to Lamont. "Read this paragraph… here… if you would."

Lamont stares at him. Faraday gives him the look: we agreed on this and you will hold to your agreement if you ever want to see Eva Tarrant again.

Lamont swallows and clears his throat, loosens his collar with his free hand and reads: "It shall be deemed that if I, Archie Connors, do not return to the ranch land called the Diamond-T for the purposes of mining along the three mile stretch within five years, that privilege shall fall to Morgan Taylor and his dependents and partners, and the lease will revert to ownership by said Morgan Taylor and his dependents and partners."

Faraday is not surprised when a loud gasp rises from the marble-like figures on the Alliance bench.

"In fact, Mr Lamont, the Taylors and the Benchleys rightfully own the three mile stretch according to the secret agreement made between your grandfather and Morgan Taylor because your grandfather did not return within five years, or at all. Morgan Taylor died and the secret agreement was never uncovered."

Lamont closes the journal. "Yes."

"What did you intend to do about that, Mr Lamont?"

"I didn't intend to kill and murder for it like…"

"Objection."

"Sustained."

"Well, Mr Lamont?"

"I was prepared to buy the three mile stretch or the whole of the Diamond-T if necessary, perhaps negotiate a similar agreement to my grandfather's, appeal to their fair and just nature, whatever, but the consortium of Bodecker, Donnelly and Parsons – the Empire you got on those maps over there – made it impossible to get near Taylor or Benchley."

"You could have written them a letter, sent a messenger, a telegram…"

Lamont shakes his head. "No."

"…something that would have alerted them to why they were being persecuted by Parsons and the danger associated with Bodecker and Donnelly."

"No."

"Why not, Mr Lamont?"

"You have to understand I was afraid for my life."

"An anonymous warning?"

"It wouldn't have done any good, I tell you."

Buchanan springs to his feet. "Your Honor, my learned colleague is badgering his own witness. For what purpose may I ask?"

"Mr Faraday," the Judge says, "would you please satisfy Mr Buchanan's curiosity?"

"I'm not badgering, Your Honor. The Alliance folk are a resourceful lot, Mr Lamont, so why wouldn't it have done any good?"

Lamont squirms. The jury is clearly riveted by his discomfort.

"The witness will answer the question," the Judge prompts.

"I had a maverick on my tail because I was trying to blackmail Bodecker."

"You were blackmailing Mr Bodecker – for what, Mr Lamont?"

"I had a maverick on my tail. Do you know how that feels, Mr Faraday?"

"Not personally, but there are several people here today who know. So, Mr Lamont, how and why were you blackmailing Mr Bodecker?"

"He... he had infiltrated another, that is, the last of my free companies. To get him out I had to attempt a boardroom maneuver. Donnelly let loose a maverick on me. I evaded a bullet twice and then lay low for a long time. I had to look after my business empire or see it fall into Bodecker's hands. I didn't have time to worry about the Alliance folk as you call them. I'm sorry for what happened to them."

"You could have used Dillon Kerr to warn them," Faraday suggests.

"Dillon is a spy; he couldn't risk his cover. I needed him to survive. You have to understand that Bodecker has his own spies, everywhere. If Dillon got caught it could have been the end of him. Mr Faraday, you must understand. We are talking about being *terrorized*. It's real and it's frightening. I'm sorry I couldn't warn the

Alliance about the danger, they appear to be nice folks, but each must look out for his own survival."

Faraday allows time to run on in silence. Then, "It wasn't because you discovered they were the owners of the three mile stretch and it no longer behooved you to be interested in what happened to it?"

Rather dejectedly, Lamont says, "I was scared, Mr Faraday. It seemed that it came down to them or me. And I chose me. I'm sorry if that don't live up the standard of legendary heroics in this town but I had to protect myself, my business empire and my employees. Bodecker ain't above killing off your workers if you don't do what he says."

"Objection."

"Overruled."

"Yeah, sure he would… if you got in his way. It happened… oh, yes, it happened to two of my girls. Shot down in the street minding their own business. A maverick followed each of them. The police couldn't ever find who did it. No one can catch a maverick. Only ones I ever heard about are the four Mr Ryan's got in his lockup…."

"Two of your girls?" Faraday asks mildly, walking towards the jury. Two or three of the jurors notice him; the rest cannot take their eyes off Lamont. In actual fact, they have wandered into unchartered territory and Faraday begins to feel his way; Lamont is just full of surprises.

"In Denver I own several palaces full of beautiful woman…"

"Palaces… You mean high class bordellos, Mr Lamont?"

The jurors sit up as one.

"Yes, that's what I mean. They are well-run and highly regarded. But Mr Bodecker and Mr Donnelly here, who don't mind transacting business in them, if you get my meaning, unleased mavericks on innocent young women. Sent a shudder through everyone; I had to focus on protecting my employees and myself."

"Have you proof that the men who killed the young women were mavericks sent by the defendants?"

Lamont swallows. "In the portfolio, the one from the safe that the marshal brought up…"

Faraday strides across the room and retrieves the portfolio.

Lamont nods. "If I may have it, I will find the proof you need."

Faraday gives the portfolio to Lamont, whose hands are trembling as he turns the pages. Finally, he stops turning and says, "Here. This is it."

Faraday takes the paper, reads the note scrawled in a familiar hand, digests its contents, and gladly hands it back to Lamont. "Read it for the court, please."

Lamont squeezes his eyes shut for a moment, then, looking a little bleary, reads. *"Kit, I warned you what would happen if you didn't back off. Now the lovelies are angels. Loren."*

The Judge taps out a warning as murmurs begin to fly.

Faraday retrieves the sheet from Lamont. "Your Honor, People's exhibit 21: a handwritten note from the defendant Loren Bodecker to the witness Kit Lamont, as proof that the defendant had two of Mr Lamont's employees murdered. I offer this into evidence, but the defense counsel has not seen it, so with your permission I will allow them to view it now."

"Very well, Mr Faraday, proceed."

Faraday puts the note to rest in front of Buchanan.

"Counselor," he says and steps away. Buchanan picks it up and glances at it. From the corner of his eye, Faraday observes Buchanan staring long and hard at his client.

"No objections, Mr Buchanan?" the Judge asks.

"None, Your Honor."

"Then continue with the witness, Mr Faraday. I ask that People's exhibit 21 be removed to the evidence table."

"Yes, Your Honor," Owens, their bailiff, readily complies.

"So, Mr Lamont, you were in quite a predicament of your own and due to fear and terror and murder in your own backyard, you could not warn the Alliance."

Lamont shakes his head. "No, sir. No, Mr Faraday. No...no..."

Fear has gripped Lamont, even now. Even with Bodecker and Donnelly in chains, the mere recollection and then giving witness to their atrocities has shaken his confidence. Faraday suspects that this cold fear of Bodecker is new to Lamont; his response to the terror he spoke of earlier was no less real, but certainly more defiant. It had to be, for his own survival. Nevertheless, it is one thing for the jury to see what cold fear does to a man, but quite another for the man himself to have to face Buchanan's cross-examination in this state.

"Mr Lamont…"

Lamont flinches and drags his gaze from his chained enemies to Faraday.

"Mr Lamont, where is the woman Eva Tarrant now?"

"Eva…" he mumbles. He wrings his hands together and frowns at them. "Eva is… she's with Dillon. I have to… to spend a month in the Territory lockup." He raises his eyes. "And then I can go find her." His gaze wanders across the room and rests on Cliff. "I hope the girl I hurt finds some… some happiness."

Faraday discreetly follows his line of sight. Cliff looks up, his blue-green gaze intense upon Lamont. Faraday wonders fleetingly why he ever doubted Cliff's wisdom in this.

"I'm sure she will, Mr Lamont," he says.

To his utter surprise, Cliff gives Lamont a somewhat contained yet undeniable smile, followed by an almost imperceptible nod. Faraday slides his eyes sidelong to catch Lamont's reaction. Calm creeps back into his expression. Reassurance. Hope.

Lamont pulls himself together, leaving Faraday to marvel at how much can be achieved over enduring nights of poker games.

"I have no further questions for Mr Lamont, Your Honor."

The Judge nods. "Your witness, Mr Buchanan."

Lamont

Under Buchanan's cross-examination

"Is it not true that your business, Mr Lamont, involves gambling, drugs and prostitution?"

"My business is as I said before. I own palaces, three of them. And I do not own gaming houses."

"Ah… I have proof, Mr Lamont, that you once owned a casino in San Francisco."

"That was my father's and he left it to me. I never wanted it, particularly since it was responsible for his death, and my mother's, so I closed it down and sold the building, with my grandfather's blessing."

"But there was a time when you made some profit from it?"

"It operated in the several weeks until I worked out what to do with it. And then it was no more."

"But you saw no vice in houses of ill-repute, did you?"

"Men work hard out here, Mr Buchanan. At first there was a scarcity of women. And men were lonely. All I did was supply some comfort and some company."

"But your palaces, as you call them, are in Denver. There is no scarcity of women in Denver these days, Mr Lamont, it is a thriving city of universal stature with a growing populace, and yet you still run houses of ill-repute."

"My palaces are clean, reputable and offer accommodation. In fact, I have an excellent reputation. I have never been closed down by the authorities for any reason…"

"How many young women do you employ, Mr Lamont?"

"In Denver, about thirty to forty."

"Young girls plucked off the street at a time in their lives when they are most vulnerable."

"Often the women have no home, or they're not wanted at home."

"Ah... the Good Samaritan."

"Some of my employees find husbands, Mr Buchanan. Mostly though, just when they think their lives might be over, they find themselves in a home and earning money. Gambling on the other hand..."

"Mr Lamont, we are not stupid people. You cannot paint a rosy picture of prostitution. The saloon girl you assaulted for example."

"Objection..."

"Overruled, Mr Faraday."

"The saloon girl, Mr Lamont. Look what happened to her. You made her black and blue."

"She doesn't belong in a saloon. Anyone can see that."

"And you would know."

"Objection."

"Sustained."

"Black and blue, Mr Lamont. She was bleeding; traumatized. "

"I heard she's gone back to her church and is going to make something of herself. Reckon I got some sense into her, even though I'm sorry I hurt her."

"Oh, you were so good for her..."

"Objection."

"Sustained."

Faraday and Ryan had prepared him well for this onslaught. Even so, it's damned uncomfortable. But like Ryan said, if Kit believed that what he did for a living was fair then don't let Buchanan put down his beliefs.

Buchanan will think he has the moral majority on his side, and he may, but you have to make the jury feel that despite what they think about what you do, you are a credible witness.

Kit didn't know how he was gonna achieve this, until Buchanan started on him and he began to understand. You stick to what you believe. And don't lie.

Buchanan hammers him for a long time on the same point – his palaces and the women he employs in them. Kit responds in the same way – like Ryan taught him – even if it means repeating himself. He tries to keep calm, no matter what Buchanan says, and he thinks of Eva, too. Every passing minute brings him one minute closer to finding her.

Then Buchanan changes his questions. Ryan warned him about this as well.

A change in questioning can trick your mind. When it happens, and you're not ready, ask Buchanan to repeat the question, or say you don't understand, until your mind has collected itself and adapted to the change.

"Mr Lamont, how did this feud between you and Mr Bodecker start?"

"Feud?"

"Yes. In your testimony you said that you and Mr Bodecker got up to some board room antics."

"A feud?"

"You know what a feud is, don't you, Mr Lamont?"

"Sure."

"So, how did this feud between you and Mr Bodecker begin?"

"I wouldn't call it a feud, Mr Buchanan. And it weren't boardroom antics neither. Mr Bodecker don't like competition. He attacked my companies one by one."

"Mr Lamont, is it true that you initiated the feud…"

"It weren't a feud, Mr Buchanan. Mr Bodecker attacked me. I did what any self-respecting businessman would do in the same situation – I fought to hold onto what was rightfully mine."

"Mr Lamont, the definition of a feud is, according to my dictionary, a bitter, long-continued and deadly quarrel."

"I had no quarrel with Mr Bodecker. I just wanted him to stop stealing my empire. We never quarreled over anything. One minute I was minding my own business and the next he comes along and starts raiding my companies…"

"But the feud between you grew bitter and long…"

"There was no feud. It was an attack. I had to fight back to stay alive."

"Mr Lamont, isn't it true that you made the first strike?"

Kit frowns.

"Come now, Mr Lamont, why so perplexed?"

"I have to say, Mr Buchanan, I don't know what you are talking about."

"Isn't it true that four years ago you presented Mr Bodecker with a young woman from one of your bordellos who laced his drink with a hallucinogenic drug and then stole all the money is his wallet?"

Kit blinks.

"Such is the quality of your whore houses, Mr Lamont."

Kit sits up. So that's what that scrawny Mead is doing here.

Mongrel.

"Have you anything to say, Mr Lamont?"

"Sure. I just had to think back some. Your information is cock-eyed, sir. Although it can happen that the girls steal from clients from time to time, in my palaces they get fired. If the women want to work for me, they know not to steal. As for the incident you just mentioned, like I said it's incorrect. I didn't own that house at the time. The old management sold out to me in October. And I did the place up quite a bit. Made it presentable and nice for guests. Brought in new staff and told them what I expected. Think you'll find that incident happened in June or July."

Kit nods reassuringly at the jury. Then he glances at Mead and watches with satisfaction as the scowl drops off his face.

"I see," says Buchanan, his voice laced with disbelief. "And what of the drugs, Mr Lamont? Isn't it true that only recently one of your women got so high on them she almost died?"

"Darla," he says flatly. "That incident you are speaking of happened when Mr Bodecker's attorney Marvin Tucker slipped a large quantity of drugs into her drink, as well as his own. Tucker brought the drugs into the house. His supplier is a friend of Mr Donnelly's – Louis Porterfield."

"All in all, Mr Lamont, the business in which you are actively engaged is morally bankrupt."

"Objection. Your Honor, my learned colleague is voicing a personal opinion, not asking a question."

"Sustained."

"You are actively engaged in your work?" Buchanan continues.

"How do you mean?"

"You test your wares, so to speak."

"Objection. Your Honor, does Mr Buchanan have a direct question, because I for one find all his innuendos unpleasant…"

"Sustained. Ask a direct question, Mr Buchanan."

"Mr Lamont, do you have sexual relations with the women you employ, and if so, do you make a habit of it, or is it a substitute for a regular job interview?"

Kit feels warm blood in his cheeks. The whole courtroom begins to buzz. This ain't good.

Don't ever panic. Take a deep breath. Think. Unravel the question word by word and ignore any images that come to mind.

Kit longs to close his eyes and blank everything and everyone out for one long, lovely minute but he knows he can't. He takes a deep breath. And thinks about the words, Ryan's as well as Buchanan's.

Remember, you believe in this, whatever anyone else might say about it.

The Judge's soft hammering to order sharpens Kit's senses.

"I have managers who employ the women. They are women themselves. New employees are put on probation and if things don't work out, we all part company friendly-like. On a regular basis I drop in to speak with the managers about the running of the business and check that standards are kept up."

"But do you take the women for your own pleasure, Mr Lamont?"

"Oh, I forgot that part of the question," he says. "Sometimes. A market owner would be foolish to sell fruit he'd never tasted himself."

Sniggers sound about the room. There was no getting around that one.

Buchanan, his voice raised, continues, "And you expect us to believe that you, Mr Lamont, are a credible witness, you who are immoral in every way?"

"Mr Buchanan, I have told you the truth, even to the point where you punish me with accusations of being immoral. I have told the truth and nothing but the truth. And as for my testimony, the reports and the journals, I could be a lying, sniveling little ferret and it would still be enough to convict your client of murder!"

Kit, the blood high in his cheeks and coursing like crazy through his veins, watches as the whole courtroom resembles pandemonium, while the Judge hammers away, calling for order.

A glance at Ryan. There's a wry smirk on his face as he goes about tapping people on the shoulder and thumbing them out of the courtroom.

Cliff

Cliff chains Lamont to his table in the interview room, aware that his poker buddy is a little weird after the cross.

"Something on your mind, Kit?"

Before Kit can answer, Mac slides a plate of food in front of him.

Cliff stands back, his arms folded across his chest. Mac gives his eyes a roll as he steps out again.

"Much obliged," Kit calls after him. He glances up. "Thanks for telling me how to handle Buchanan."

"We all want the same thing. Unfortunately, he hasn't finished with you. Lucky for you the Judge got hungry."

Cam appears in the doorway, a curious light in his eyes.

"You did well, Mr Lamont."

Kit picks up his fork and starts poking at the hot stew in front of him. "What should I expect after lunch, Mr Faraday?"

"I'm not sure, Mr Lamont," he says and looks across at Cliff. "Buchanan and Sturrock have met with me and have requested another meeting before we resume. We have time."

While Cliff's heart begins to beat faster, Kit pokes about in his stew and says, "Whatever makes you happy, Mr Faraday."

Cam gives a laugh. "Enjoy your lunch, Mr Lamont."

They walk out, leaving Kit with his stew.

"Are you about to tell me we have plea bargain?" Cliff says after closing the door to his office.

"They floated one."

"And?"

"Donnelly – life imprisonment with solitary confinement and hard labor, never to be released."

"He's a killer, Cam. It's a proven fact now. People will be expecting him to hang. Surely his fate is sealed, regardless of trying to escape a hanging by clinging to Bodecker's coat tails."

"I am not disagreeing with any of what you just said. Although I don't want you telling me what you think I want to hear."

"I know. I won't. What about Bodecker?"

"The black suits are willing to take life with hard labor with his admission of guilt and thorough allocution."

"Are they now? And Bodecker? What is he willing to take?"

Cam sighs. "Murder for hire, conspiracy to murder... the endless list of crimes... He is among the very worst of men."

"Remember when Wilson Cutter confessed? – he had that hellfire preacher in his ear..."

"Jamison... I remember. He left town not long after."

"Cutter's last request was that his hanging not be public; he wanted to meet his maker in private. Jamison walked him to the scaffold."

Cam pulls up a chair. "I remember Ethan asked me if I thought Cutter deserved a final request... and John Keaton said that Mart would agree with the reverend, and it didn't matter what we would think. This was Mart's justice after all."

Cutter's hanging is vivid in Cliff's memory.

What is also crystal clear in his memory regarding Cutter's hanging on that misty morning last fall is his conversation with Emma about it, and her reaction to his asking if she had ever seen anyone hanged. The pain in her eyes struck him in the heart when she answered... she'd seen innocence, justice and the constitution of a free people hanged on a tree, she said; she'd seen too much hanging to justify any more hanging at all.

Time we stop hanging folks.

He clears his throat, wondering how he will ever be able to forget her, pushing down the wave of despair he feels rising up inside him. He says what Cam *needs* to hear. "Hanging is too good for Bodecker, but stripped of all his possessions, which have all gone to his victims, a life sentence of hard labor would likely finish him, and grind that mean arrogance of his into dust."

This leaves Cam to take this conversation where it was always headed. "You think I should talk to the Alliance."

"We've come this far. Every step of the way with them."

"I'm curious, Sheriff Ryan, will it matter to you either way?"

Under Cam's good-natured scrutiny, Cliff shifts his feet and thinks about what he's lost in pursuit of justice for Miss Keaton and bringing to an end Bodecker's murderous regime.

And what he has gained.

His new religion teaches mercy and forgiveness. Encourages pity. Revenge is not justice. Life and death relate to the condition of your soul as well as the condition of your body. And no one has the right to take the life of another. He would hear the bastards' pathetic confessions and tolerate their continued presence on earth rather than watch them hang. And in a way execution was letting them take the easy way out; they deserved extreme punishment and the excruciation of looking true remorse in the eye and then seeing their hideous selves staring back at them. Could they do it? And could all those they'd hurt find some measure of peace as a result of such a prospect?

Remorse and forgiveness equal peace, Cliff, remember that if you can, there's a good man... never enough peace in this world, but hope has not forsaken us...

Even when every minute of the day unhappiness is the only flavor you can taste in your mouth?

Emma was happiness.

There is no Emma.

She may have forsaken him but not hope apparently.

He remembers Cam is still sitting there and looks up.

Cam brows are knit together. "You really can't do this job any more, can you?" He stands up and goes to the door. "I'll talk to Luke and the others now. Drop by the Governor. I'll be in my office afterwards, waiting for the black suits."

"Cam... I haven't given up on this case."

"Oh, don't worry," Cam says, opening the door and grinning, "I never thought that for a second."

Faraday

The Cheyenne Hotel is busy with lunchtime customers; half the dining room is taken up by the Alliance, having maneuvered several tables into a collective. All bar none sit in a kind of stupor, although as he approaches he notices George and Luke are not among them.

"Mr Faraday," Amy Keaton greets him, "please join us…"

John begs the pardon of a couple at a nearby table and nabs their unused chair, placing it next to Amy's, and Faraday is eagerly invited to sit. They all stare at him with questions in their eyes.

He smiles. "I know this has all been a huge shock."

"There's gotta be a better word than shock for how I feel," John says dryly.

"I'm here for a specific purpose…"

"Go ahead, Cam," Ben Taylor says; beside him, Raina smiles her confident agreement.

Faraday nods. "The black suits want a specific meeting before the session resumes…"

"They want to discuss a plea bargain?" asks Ben, his tone incredulous.

"A plea bargain, yes. The testimony of Mr Lamont and the evidence are damning."

"Damn them all to hell," Richard Taylor mutters.

"Mr Taylor, I was very glad to see you in court this morning," Faraday says. "It couldn't have been easy to sit in the same room with Bodecker after all he put you through."

"I won't have people talking about me behind my back."

"I understand," Faraday says, smiling.

"We're not afraid, Mr Faraday," Caroline remarks.

"I've never known a single one of you to show nothing less than astounding courage. But... what I want to know is do you expect..."

"A hanging? For each?" John cuts in, and Amy wraps her fingers around her husband's arm.

"We expected they would be found guilty and the Judge would decide their sentence," she says.

"I'm not sure there is anything substantial their lawyers can put forward in their defense at this stage. Unless we have slipped up somewhere. However, if Buchanan and Sturrock want to bargain for the lives of their clients with a full admission of guilt by them, then I'm certain they believe the jury will otherwise convict and the sentence will be hanging. Their only job now is to see to it that they don't hang."

All stare blankly at him.

"So, what are your thoughts, your expectations?"

Ethan says, "Seems to me we've been through something like this before."

John clears his throat. "We said we would do what Mart would have wanted. But this seems different. Seems so much bigger."

"In many ways it is, but the reason we began this journey together remains at the core of it. I am, and always have been, acutely aware of the priceless value of your daughter's life." How could he not be with his own precious new daughter at home? "I know this is all so much to take in."

"You would make them publicly confess, wouldn't you, Cam?" Ben asks.

"In court, every foul deed and false word, and I would have to be thoroughly satisfied. I will not let them rest until I am."

"Foul and false indeed," Caroline mutters.

"I will need to speak with Luke. Where is he?"

"He and Jennifer went straight home," Sara Taylor replies. "He's very upset."

"I wouldn't be too upset if I found out I owned a gold mine, even if my father had lied about it," Ben remarks.

"Yeah, well, you're used to your father being an inconceivable louse," Ethan retorts.

They gasp as one, and one or two napkins are hurled in his direction. And even as Caroline is saying, "Ethan Benchley, you take that back," Richard himself barks a laugh at his own expense.

None of this is helpful. Such behavior can only be the result of shock and strain. He needs to talk to Luke. He stands up to excuse himself.

"Mr Faraday..."

"Yes, John?"

"There's been a lot of killing, d'you really think we need more? For anyone's sake? No matter what anyone does or doesn't believe in?" Those eyes of renowned Keaton-blue shimmer. In spite of everything, Faraday sees hope in their depths.

"At this point I would rightly say, the Law will decide. But if that were true in this case I wouldn't be here. I believe I understand you, John...Amy." And before he takes his leave he reminds them all, "No reporters."

"You have our word," Ethan replies.

George opens the door to him.

"Cam," she says and hugs him. The hug is welcome, particularly as she adds, "You are so clever, you have done a wonderful job..."

Most people wrongly assume he doesn't need to hear this. George is not most people. "Thank you." He pats her back, looking over her shiny chestnut head to Luke seated at the table.

"Have you eaten?" she asks, drawing him inside and closing the door.

"Too busy," he replies, taking the chair opposite Luke.

"Have some?" Luke offers.

There's a plate of cold-cuts sandwiched between surgically sliced bread on the table between them.

"We just made them," Luke expands. "Bread's fresh."

Faraday observes the exhaustion pinching Luke's face and takes a sandwich.

"How did you spend the night, Cam?" George asks, pouring him coffee.

"I do not know what we would do without Constance. I believe Meg may be changing her mind about that one," he says reaching for a napkin.

"And the baby?"

He thinks of the tiny bundle of perfection and smiles inwardly, while dreams of her long and happy life sing in his head. "Lily is doing just fine." He places his sandwich on his napkin. "There's something I need to talk to you about. I've spoken to the others. I believe I know where they stand on the issue, but as for you…"

"Go on."

Luke's dark eyes regard him steadily, almost as if he knows what's coming.

"Buchanan and Sturrock have asked for a meeting before we go back into court. They will want to plea bargain for Bodecker and Donnelly's lives."

Luke shifts in his seat. "I see."

"It's almost something you forget," George murmurs, "the sentence… I mean, you work so hard for the conviction, but… by law, they should hang, shouldn't they?"

"We have a water-tight case. Lamont's testimony along with the evidence he had in his possession sealed it. I doubt there is anything Buchanan can do at this point. I'm trying to ascertain if you want this, Luke. Do you want them to hang?"

"It ain't up to me, Cam. You know the law."

"Yes, but…"

"Besides, won't the Governor have something to say about it?"

"I have seen Governor Warren; before I came here in fact. The political fall-out from this will not be pretty either way; no one in the Governor's office saw Bodecker coming. What they did see was the enormous progress and the prosperity he created, and I believe this has swayed him. Cliff and I pursued Bodecker aware that it could ruin our careers and our reputations. We believed in the Alliance, in all of you, and that faith has never been betrayed. The

Governor basically said as much to me a few minutes ago. He respects the Alliance and he regrets deeply what has happened. Look, to cut this short, he will not interfere with either sentence or plea bargain, no matter the objections or the protestations."

"You mean to tell me, Cam, the Governor thinks people owe Bodecker something?"

"It's the age-old partnership, prosperity and corruption, strange bedfellows and shades of gray. But, equally, he thinks he owes the Alliance something too."

He looks unconvinced. "What about the law in all this?"

"Certainly, the crimes committed by Bodecker and Donnelly are punishable by hanging, but also by life imprisonment with hard labor, not a well-used option I grant you. Still, it is in my power to have them publicly admit to everything they did, abjectly apologize, have them watch as their ill-gotten gains are carved up to financially compensate their victims, and have them sentenced to life in prison with hard labor, never to be released.

"And, it is in my power to proceed with the trial to its conclusion and see the jury convict them; they would be hanged. The black suits are seeking to pre-empt the inevitable by having that sentence commuted before it's been handed down. And they know that if they tried to appeal such sentence, they would not succeed. So they will plea for the lives of their clients.

"Luke, I believe that in this case the plea bargain should not be directed solely at the office of the district attorney, and frankly if anyone has any objection they can go jump in the lake. You wanted justice. You have fought damn hard for it. You almost died for it. What do *you* want to see done?"

"Cam, I don't think you should be asking me what's to be done with them."

"So happens I am. I know many people believe that hanging is too good for Donnelly, but there is the other view, and a valid one, that in prison he would suffer greatly, terribly, condemned to live out the rest of his life in harsh remorse and self-pity for his crimes. He is already showing signs that incarceration would be more than he could bear. So should he hang or should he endure a lifetime of torture?"

Silence. Eyes down.

"Luke, I saw the photographs. I have some inkling of what he put you through…"

"It's not me," he says. Another difficult silence follows. At last he says, "I have to think of K, what she would want."

"I know you do. But they almost killed every one of you."

"Almost," he concurs and looks up. "Part of me wants to be rid of them forever, but the other part knows it won't sit right if I don't do what K would want."

"What is that?" George asks.

He looks at her, whereupon his eyes soon grow damp and glisten as sadness and grief well up from the deep place where he usually keeps them. "She'll haunt me forever if I was to insist they hang for what they did to her. But they did it to Mart, too. And she loved him more than anything."

"So, she would want what Mart would want," George reasons carefully. "Justice, not revenge."

He gives a nod. "Confronting remorse and damnable self-pity, trapped, caged and living with despair, because that's the hard part, that's when they would know the pain, and God knows I want them to hurt in the worst way."

"Is *that* what you want, Luke?" Faraday asks. "Because no one will haunt you, no one will judge if you want Bodecker and Donnelly to swing at the end of a noose. No one would dare."

"For me merely *wanting* them to hang she would dare haunt me. My crime for her was always my lack of sincerity, the purity of my intentions, don't you see?"

It's a little chilling, the extent to which he believes what he just said. Faraday fights the inclination to look over his shoulder for the ghost of Miss Keaton.

"No, I don't. Pardon me for saying so, but you mustn't ever think that because it's wrong and Miss Keaton clearly didn't understand you very well."

"In K's world everything was black and white."

"That couldn't have been easy."

"It wasn't. What did John and Amy say?"

Faraday wonders when he'd ask that. "That there has been

enough killing, and, they led me to believe Miss Keaton didn't agree with capital punishment."

"Guess not. But I know for a fact she thought about Cutter hanging for what he did to Mart. It was fleeting, but she thought it. As we looked on the gallows, she said *is it wrong to want to watch Cutter hang from there?*"

Faraday remembers the two of them in those tense moments before Luke made his uncompromising stand to foil Wilson Cutter's extradition. The recollection brings a lump to his throat.

"And what did you say?"

"I said, I thought it was normal, because to go beyond that desire and desire mercy instead was to reach another level of humanity. And she said, *the level where people are able to imitate the Divine?*"

"So is that what we are doing when we spare criminals the noose?"

"When you think about it I guess."

Faraday sighs. "But we are only human after all."

"I know, but I swore, Cam, on that hill in San Francisco, watching the ships and the gulls and the wind whipping the sea, that I would live the honorable life that Mart and K died for, whatever that meant, whatever it took."

"But none of us knew then what we know now, how far this went, how many would be killed."

"I'm not even sure I'm the same person who made that vow. How can I be? It seems so long ago…"

Faraday exchanges glances with George. Her expression reflects the discomfort in Luke's voice, and a certain degree of helplessness. He needs to break the tension, give Luke more time to deal with the emergence of Miss Keaton's memory. "I'm very sorry about your father."

Luke sits back. "You don't have to commiserate about that, Cam, it ain't your job."

"Our parents keep secrets from us."

"Your father owns a gold mine, Cam?" he says flippantly.

"No, but after my mother died he told me that he'd been married before. He was very young and the marriage was annulled.

When I accused him of keeping secrets from me, he said, what did it have to do with me?"

"I… I understand what you're saying, but my father drummed our heritage story into my head since I was a baby. This is who you are, he would say. Be proud and remember."

"So you should. And look at the fascinating chapter you have to add to it."

"Yes, but how do I know if *any* of it is genuine?"

"I guess facing the truth about our past can be an unpalatable task. I remember when Miss Keaton and I were swapping letters in the Bugle and finally you became incensed enough to write one of your own. You accused her of having a romanticized notion of liberty and property."

"She never understood the concept of liberty and property; she had it wrong," he says, shaking his head.

"Be that as it may, it seems to me she held the realist viewpoint. And you, my friend, are the romantic."

Luke throws a laugh. "I remember that letter. She made me so mad… *How much blood has been spilled across this continent in the last one hundred years, and now from one ocean to another we say we are free.* How did she think of that, I used to wonder, and then I realized it was because she wasn't saddled with heritage. She could see things from a truly free position. We'd argue about freedom and independence. I would never budge from the position my father expected of me. My forefathers fought for freedom in this country, and what did she do? – she accused all of us of being as bad as the ones we fought against. One empire to replace the other."

"Mm, sounding very like a certain reporter we all know," Faraday says.

"Dear Emmaline," George says with a smile. "Everyone works or fights to keep their patch of Empire. Bodecker's empire nearly swallowed up the Alliance empire, but you fought for it, same as your forefathers fought to take the colonies from the British, the same as the Indian nations fought to stave off the whites, and aren't we here in Cheyenne because they lost?"

Luke gives her a gentle nod. "They come and they go, empires. I guess they always will, no matter what anyone believes in."

A long silence ensues, wherein all the words take their places and settle into thought. There is no limit to Faraday's time and patience when it comes to Luke and George, and so he waits.

At length, Luke says, "Getting back to the plea bargain."

"Yes…"

"If you're asking me…"

"I am."

"If you want us to be a part of your decision…"

"I think justice demands it."

"I only hope, Cam, you're not doing this because you feel guilty about what happened…" – when Faraday failed to act upon Miss Keaton recognizing Bodecker's face in Luke's file.

Faraday regards him with affection. "Can't a friend make reparation?"

"You gotta uphold the law, Cam."

"Of course. Always."

"Then the only people you owe anything to are John and Amy. The loss is theirs; justice belongs to them. The rest of us were only fighting to make sure they got it."

Faraday feels a tingle at the back of his neck. And he wonders: has Miss Keaton just made her approval known? He shakes it off and gets to his feet.

"Then that shall be my guide."

"Don't forget this," George says, hastily wrapping his sandwich in his napkin. She lays it in the palm of his hand.

He grins at her. "Yes, Doctor."

Judge's chambers

Judge Callaghan is slowly gowning himself in readiness for the afternoon session.

"Mr Faraday, how are you?" he says in such a tone as to suggest he'd eaten a good lunch. "Ventured home to take another peek at that baby daughter of yours, eh?"

"Ah…"

"I'm dying to take a peek at her myself," he enthuses while smoothing his hair.

Faraday thinks it must have been a very good lunch. "You are always welcome, Judge. Why don't you call on Sunday. I'm sure Meg will be on hand by then…"

"Excellent suggestion. Now…"

"Yes, Judge. Buchanan and Sturrock have requested a meeting before we proceed."

"Oh?" says the Judge, putting on his spectacles. "And you know what it's about?"

"They want to discuss a plea bargain."

"I see. Certainly, we have reached an interesting juncture in the case." He peers over the top of his spectacles. "If it goes as you expect, I will call an adjournment until Monday morning."

"Yes, Judge."

"Mr Faraday…"

"Yes, Judge?"

"We have a county lockup to clear out. I want it done."

Buchanan

"Are you sure there is nothing we can do?" Sturrock asks.

Buchanan shakes his head. "The damage done by Lamont can't be mended. The jury saw what kind of man he is, and it didn't rattle them. As for the evidence…"

Sturrock sighs hard. "Nothing Mead has can match it?"

"Not a thing. Lamont is too forthright. Someone has trained him too cleverly on how to deliver his responses, probably Ryan."

"But between the two of us we could break him."

"And have the jury feel sorry for a pimp and a rapist? Sturrock, let's face it. There are few to none who will stand up for Loren at this point. He has been brought to his knees and so now they are no longer scared of him. As for Donnelly…"

"The less said the better."

"Precisely. But as long as he remains in Loren's wagon, he'll survive. It's a long shot, but I think I know Faraday well enough. You, too. This is the only way, all that's left."

They nod in agreement, move out of their huddle and cross the room to where their clients keep company with their uneaten lunch.

"Gentlemen, Faraday's messenger will be here soon. Are you ready for this?"

Donnelly looks up, hands shaking. "I didn't get my chance…"

"Don't be deceived, Mr Donnelly," Buchanan says, "we are to bargain; it doesn't mean that Faraday will accept our offer. You may still get your chance. And if you do, you will surely hang!"

Loren grunts. "Even I know you wouldn't let him anywhere near the witness stand. Look at him, fucking disappointment."

"I'm looking at you, Loren," Buchanan retorts.

"Huh! Don't you think I'll look pretty at the end of a hangman's noose?"

"No one does. You sink or swim together, gentlemen. It's the only way. And if this works, it's because Sturrock and I have tapped into an element in this trial you two couldn't begin to understand."

Loren looks bored with the answer. "Any word on Parsons?"

Sturrock sighs. "He's back in the hospital wing."

"Dying?"

"It seems that way."

"All he wanted was that quartz ore."

"Well, it didn't belong to him," Buchanan mutters.

"I want to take my chance with the jury!" Loren declares.

"We can't do that and get a desirable outcome, Loren."

"Quit with that tone of voice, Buchanan. Talk to me like I belong in an asylum again and I'll fire you and get someone else."

He and Sturrock exchange glances; they've both had enough.

Loren is still ranting…"This is all your fault, Donnelly."

Donnelly turns a paler shade of white than he is already. If his nerves were fraying before the fire, they're unravelling now. For a man capable of extreme violence and cruelty, his cowardly ways are quite the revelation. Still, he has enough of the nasty left in him to say, "If you had only let Maverick deal with them all when we began the consortium…"

"Shut up," Loren hisses.

"…this would never have happened. Instead you had to make sport with them."

"Me make sport? You mean little prick, I ought to… "

"Enough!" Sturrock barks.

Donnelly begins to sob; before long, his nose and eyes are running. What next?

"We will do what we can," Buchanan tells them, tossing a handkerchief into Donnelly's manacled hands.

Loren looks disgusted and turns his head away.

There's comes a sharp rap on the door; one of McNamara's prison guards opens it, pushes his grim head inside and announces that Faraday will see them in his office.

Faraday

Faraday stands at the window and waits; won't be long now.

Soon enough, his office door opens and Josh admits Buchanan and Sturrock.

"Gentlemen…"

"Faraday," Buchanan says.

Sturrock nods.

"Won't you sit down…?"

And they do.

Buchanan looks down at his hands. And back up again.

Sturrock tugs at his necktie before straightening it.

Faraday wonders if he picked up that particular habit from Donnelly as he says, "So, gentlemen, let's get down to business."

Jennifer

DEAR JENNIFER, RECEIVED LONG LETTER FROM JOSEPH. DERMOT WILL NOT LAST MUCH LONGER. JOE THINKS HE IS WAITING FOR YOU. IF YOU WANT TO GO YOU MUST GO NOW. LOVE FRANK.

Luke lowers the telegram. As bewildered as he looks, at least he can't accuse her of keeping it from him, like the last one from Frank. This is even more urgent than that.

He's not sleeping soundly, so he's exhausted as well as drained after yesterday. Ease him into the idea, would be Frank's advice.

"I know the timing couldn't be worse…"

"That's an understatement."

"It's unfortunate and out of my control."

He shifts his feet; gathers a frown across his brow. He's onto her. "All right, sweetheart, you need to tell me what's going on here. This arrived five minutes ago, we've read the darn old thing and now something's changed. "

"You know how some things are. Sometimes they're quick…"

"Just tell me."

"I…I'm going… to Provincetown…tomorrow."

"Tomorrow? But, Jennifer, I can't leave now."

"I know. You… *you* cannot leave now, but *I* can."

"You want to leave without me…?"

"It's not a question of what I want."

"Go without me…?"

"How could you think I would want either of those things? I don't *want* to go without you, or leave you, but it seems to me every day counts where Dermot is concerned. The rest of the world is not running to Judge Callaghan's court schedule."

"That ain't fair."

"Luke, this is *my* decision. If it were up to you I wouldn't go at all, yet it's because of you that I can do this. Remember, we agreed that Dermot must have loved me at some point, while..."

"He and your mother were waiting for you to be born, sure, but..."

"That's right. So, if he did love me once, loved me enough to bring me into being, and subsequently force my life in your direction, then perhaps I should perform this one last goodbye. I know you think I'm being ridiculous, and I do not love him, or respect him, or want to see him, but when I think of my mother, who loved Dermot and me the way I love you and Evan, then I feel I must to do it for her. She died on account of me. All I have of my parents, Luke, is the moments after I was born, when my mother was still alive. I have nothing else... nothing..."

Self-pity or sadness or grief, whatever it is she feels, seizes her; she cannot contain it. She feels herself breaking into tiny pieces, each one saturated with heavy tears, so heavy she wants to fall to the ground. Through the long years, she held it back, that pain, and the rage against the unfairness of it all, but now the dam wall is collapsing. Her eyes swell with tears and spill over. "When my mama died she had no idea she was leaving her precious newborn baby to the abuse Dermot inflicted on me. She thought he would love and cherish me. And he betrayed her trust. How horrible is that? I cannot think of her and not think of that."

He seems oblivious to her distress. "You said you couldn't do this without me."

How can he not understand? Frank warned her Luke was not yet mature enough to handle the complexity of her situation; small steps, Frank said; she would have to be strong enough for both of them until he found his way, Frank said; and he will, Frank said.

Right. It's time to grow up. No holding back now. No mollycoddling. She is in dire distress and must worry about *his* feelings?

"You could be standing right by my side when I see Dermot and I would still have to do it myself."

"You speak of it like death," he says, grasping her shoulders.

His intuition is as sharp as ever.

"Am I not dying to myself to do this?"

"You said you wouldn't leave…"

"I know what I said," she argues. "But I must do this and you must stay here, secure our future and complete everything for which you have worked so hard and sacrificed so much."

"I need to come with you. I can't simply…"

"You're not listening to me, Luke."

"Believe me, I'm listening."

"But with ears only attune to what they want to hear. I will leave on the morning train to Denver."

"No…"

"You cannot stop me."

"You only have to wait a few more days and…"

"Then follow in a few more days."

"You cannot do this." And he backs away from her.

"Luke, we have come so far. You do not need to fear this."

"I'm not afraid."

"Yes, you are."

"You don't understand. You and Evan are the only things in this world keeping me sane and you are leaving…"

"You know perfectly well there is nothing wrong with you. *Nothing*. You are perfectly sane. Perfectly."

"Then how am I supposed to take care of you?"

"I told you. By finishing what you started and securing our future. That is taking care of me. What I have to do is about death and conclusion. What you do, what you have always done, is be the source of all my hope."

He emits an angry, frustrated exclamation.

"I'm sorry," she says. "I know this is hard…"

Again, he sighs harshly.

"…but I need to put this to rest."

"And if something happens to you?"

"I'm a seasoned traveler and I can take care of myself."

"You are carrying our child."

"So? I will keep Evan safe. Do you think for one minute I would put our child at risk? What a ridiculous notion. When I think of the... that he is part of... I wish you would grow up, Luke, just grow up."

The last bit slipped out. Was meant to be thought but not said. At least not that way. But it's all out now and can't be taken back.

"Now look what you made me say! Enough! I have said all I care to say. Why can't you be reasonable?" She glares at him before she leaves the room and charges upstairs to their bedroom.

"Jennifer..." he calls after her, but there is a whine of defeat about it that irritates her and fuels her distress.

She finds her suitcase in the closet, throws it open on the bed and begins tossing undergarments from her top drawer into the cavity. "Immature, pig-headed, chauvinistic... Take care of me? What am I, a baby?" From subsequent drawers she whisks out several articles of clothing and lays them on the bed. "Ridiculous, immature..." Her travel clothes hang in the cupboard; hatbox on the shelf above. "Immature, short-sighted..." Gloves, muffler, shoes.

When the time comes, remember this. Deal? The next time you doubt that I love you more than anything else in the world.

He wasn't being immature then. He was trying to win her back. Smooth the rough waters.

Movement catches her eye. He has arrived at the bedroom door. Disappointment weighs heavy in his features as he surveys her packing.

She is his sweetheart, his whole world, and she's leaving him to do something she promised she would never do without him.

What else can she do?

He is only a man after all, she can hear Meg say, what do you honestly expect; they don't get it, Jen, you know that; just get on with it and he'll get over it, or decide to not get over it and have to live without you – which do you think he would choose? You, of course, every time, so get on with it!

She is certainly blessed to have so many wise people in her life.

"I'll see about supper," he mumbles. "You... you finish what you're doing and get some rest."

Without a backward glance, he's gone. His footsteps sound quick and heavy on the stairs and a moment later the backdoor slams shut.

She slumps on the bed, telling herself to be calm while he grows used to the idea. Exhausted, she finally lays herself down; she takes his pillow and holds it to her, pressing her face into the linen to breathe his scent. She places her cheek against it and closes her eyes. *Small steps, he will find his way…*

The dark of evening has fallen when she wakes; the lamp glows softly on her dressing table on the other side of the room. Supper is cooking, its tasty aroma arousing her hunger.

Luke has covered her with the throw rug and piled her packing neatly onto his side of the bed. She freshens up and makes herself presentable, and when she reaches the bottom of the stairs he is piling food on two plates… steak, fried potato and onions. A strange meal for a man who owns a gold mine, except that he cooks a 'mean steak', as Ethan says. The red meat is good for her condition. And she can manage the onions because they are soft and disappear into the crushed, semi-crispy potatoes. She loves this simple, mouth-watering meal, and he knows it.

"I was about to wake you," he says, returning the pan to the stove. "Are you hungry?"

She could eat a banquet and still have room for his steak and fried potatoes.

"Yes."

"Sit down." He pulls her chair for her, makes sure she's comfortable. As she takes up her knife and fork, he puts a plate of freshly sliced bread on the table. Already the steak juices are mingling with the potatoes. He always says he doesn't like that; he prefers them separate and to leave the juice for the bread. She, on the other, likes everything to take on a bit of everything else…

He pours water into both their glasses, sits down and they eat.

The meal is so delicious that the unusual silence between them is bearable. Just. Two people eating a simple meal contains more complexities of noise and activity than a person realizes; when there is little to no conversation it is surprisingly noticeable.

He clears the plates.

"That was wonderful."

"Thanks. Dessert?"

"What dessert?"

"Signora Severini dropped it by while you were sleeping…"

As he busies himself, she asks, "Are the Severinis truly going to work on the Diamond-T?"

"Apparently. Ethan's hired them. Tip's promised to teach the boys how to ranch and Signora will be the new cook."

"What about your old cook?"

"Not our grub cook; Tom wouldn't be too happy losing his job."

"What then?" she asks to his back.

"She will help Tom out, but mainly cook for Ethan and Tip, and…"

"And?"

He turns around holding two bowls of a rich looking dessert.

"What is that?"

"Don't know what it's called. All I know is that it tastes good."

He places one before her and sits himself down with the other. He takes up his spoon and starts scooping up what appears to be layers of whipped cream, meringue, sponge and fruit pieces.

"I can smell alcohol."

"A smidgeon, Signora said. In the sponge apparently."

"Smidgeon? That doesn't sound very Italian."

He gives a laugh and puts it in his mouth.

"You didn't answer me before. Signora will cook for Ethan and Tip and…?"

He swallows, puts down his spoon, and looks at her.

Her heart starts beating very fast.

"It doesn't matter," he says quietly, his eyes glittering.

"What are you doing?"

"Saying something. I can't promise my behavior at the depot tomorrow will be very mature."

She feels her cheeks go warm with regret. He'd heard her.

He scoops more of Signora's lush dessert onto his spoon and shoves it into his mouth. When it's swallowed, he says, "I went out.

Saw Cliff and asked him to meet us at the depot tomorrow. He agreed to stop me from getting on the train with you."

She frowns. "Would you explain that for me?"

"It doesn't matter how angry or disappointed I am right now, tomorrow when you step onto the train, the thing that binds me to you will start to pull, and pull hard, and when the train starts to move away, it will pull my heart right out of my chest and to stop it from happening I'll need to get on the train. But then the only thing to stop me from getting on the train will be Cliff, holding onto me."

She looks down at her portion, devastated. "I... I know I promised I would never leave you, but I have to break it, and I'm sorry. Sometimes that happens with promises."

"There is a lot to do here, now and after the trial, so I don't know when I will be able to follow you," he responds with a touch of unfamiliar coldness in his voice. "You were right. Seems I have some growing up to do. You can't baby me about this Dermot business any longer."

She lifts her gaze. The look in his eyes also seems detached.

"When you come to think of it," he continues, "recalling what you said about doing this alone even if I was standing right beside you, there's no sense in both of us going, is there? Never been any reason for me to go at all."

"That was mean, Luke. I'm the one with the past, remember? If either of us should be insecure, it should be me. Or are you suddenly vying for the position?"

He doesn't reply, staring at her with those detached eyes.

"I thought you loved me more than anything else in the world. I thought I was your world. That's what you told me. You said I had to remember it, always. Has it changed?"

"No."

"Then stop making this worse than it is."

His eyelids blink several times. "I will, I promise."

"It has to be done. And we will get through it."

She half expects him to shrug and murmur sulkily *if you say so*, because her frustration with him is giving her voice a defensive edge that would make anyone want to walk away.

Instead, with a stoicism that would make Meg chuckle, he says,

"I'll be waiting for you, right here, when you return. I trust that Evan will be safe. You will work things out with Dermot; you will succeed like you always do, and then you'll come back."

"And why wouldn't I come home to my husband, the father of my child? Luke, you have to believe that it will all work out in the end. You taught me not to be afraid of life, why are you suddenly the one who's scared?"

Now the shrug. "I don't know, maybe because my whole life has been turned on its head and now my wife is leaving me."

Small steps. He will find his way.

One can only hope.

Contrarily, the night brings him trying to change her mind; but not with words, since they didn't work for him. In sort of a way, she finds his efforts rather endearing. But her course of action is fixed, and, whether he intended to or not, he has given her what she needed to undertake it – his love. She must not pity him his disappointment that, despite his best efforts, making love to her won't get him his own way.

She wakes early to find him already arisen. She hears him downstairs, probably fixing breakfast. She reaches out and touches his cold pillow.

The aroma of good, strong coffee lifts her spirits. And he has toasted bread and scrambled eggs.

"How are you?" he asks, pouring her coffee.

She waits until he puts the coffee pot down and then places her arms around him. He's unshaven, although it's hardly more than a shadow, and again looks as though he barely slept. His arms gather her up, however; then he strokes her hair down to its tips. He looks in her eyes, offers a sad, philosophical smile and kisses her lips.

This is them. And very soon they will be far apart. This Dermot Mountain has to be conquered once and for all, or they will never see the valley of plenty, that sweet land of liberty, on the other side.

Luke

Sunday

Meg shows far more understanding than he did or ever could. She hugs and kisses Jennifer goodbye, fusses that they will see each other soon, and reassures her that Constance is taking excellent care of them all. Even Cam seems pleased she is going off to do battle with Dermot; he hugs her, too, and tells her she is doing the right thing. Luke resents that. Before he knows it, they have fifteen minutes to get to the depot and say their goodbyes.

The engine hisses a lot as it prepares to leave.

It is actually happening and he can't stop it. He may as well be in Porterfield's basement for all the say he has in this. In contrast to his pitiful state, she has an air about her; strength of purpose, yes.

"Say something," she whispers, green eyes bleeding concern.

More words? He's said all there is; his power of speech is numb like the rest of him. He's cooked for her, argued with her, and made love to her, whether to change her mind or to say goodbye he's not sure, but she took it as goodbye.

"Say what?"

"I love you."

There's that; he was trying to avoid it. Too much emotion. Still, he should say it. "Love you back."

"And wish me a safe journey."

That, too. Of course he wants her to be safe. But he has no control over a single thing, so why say it?

He nods brusquely. Says it anyway. "Be safe."

61

The engine-whistle sounds.

He gazes at her until an imprint of her face is all he can see, so her living image will be constant and fresh to his eyes.

"Goodbye, Jennifer."

Her kiss lingers on his cheek; her lips are pressed against his. He wants to pull away but can't deny her or himself that last taste of heaven. Immature he may be, but this is self-preservation.

He sees her safely aboard.

"Don't worry about us," she says, "we will be fine, I promise."

Her promises are looking a little thin at this point, but he gives her a firm nod of approval.

The whistle sounds again and the conductor is pacing the platform ordering people about.

He steps back, signaled firmly by the conductor. The train begins to roll. Panic surges inside him; he hangs his head hoping to cap it by not looking, but it bubbles and gurgles and then gushes to the surface. His head bobs up.

Why are you letting her do this?

His insides feel like a thousand stampeding cattle. The train is moving off, stammering, hiccupping, gathering momentum, leaving him behind.

Don't worry about us… about us… about us…

Something disturbs the air beside him.

A hand comes down on his shoulder. And a voice with a self-mocking edge to it says, "At least yours wants you to follow her later, pal."

The butt of the train passes by him, leaving chilled steam in its wake. He can't be sure whether the hand on his shoulder is pulling him back or if he is yearning towards the train. The effect is the same; he's going nowhere.

And that voice, one he knows in the depths of turmoil, quips, "Looks like we've both got that long problem again…"

Oh, he remembers that feeling all too well. He wallows in it for some *long* moments.

He glances sidelong at Cliff, who is watching the train disappear with a more philosophical expression.

"Least I didn't run after the train."

Cliff looks at him and laughs; gives him a shake before he drops his hand. "It was touch and go."

"I should have tried harder to stop her."

"And if Dermot dies and she regrets not going, she might resent you for it all her life and you'd feel a whole lot worse, believe me."

But if anything happens to her...

"Gone with her... Would that have been so bad?"

"Can't say it would have, but that's not what she wanted, is it?"

"No. Not what she wanted. And I can't stand self-pity."

"Neither can I. So, I have some expensive whiskey a friend gave me, and we can try and drown it, if you want to drop by later."

Faraday

Monday morning, day fifteen of the trial
Judge Callaghan has locked down the courtroom
Only court personnel are allowed to come and go

"Mr Faraday, are the People satisfied with Mr Donnelly's allocution of all his criminal activities?"

"We are, Your Honor."

"Then, Mr Sturrock, you will please instruct your client to now make his apology and announce his reparations."

"Yes, Your Honor."

Sturrock leans across, passing a second sheet of paper into Donnelly's hand, whispering to him. Donnelly's hand trembles so violently he cannot keep the page sufficiently still to read from it. Sturrock takes it back and holds it for him. His voice is not much better than his hand, as he splutters and stammers…

"I, Terrence Donnelly, make a full, unreserved and sincere apology to the Keaton, the Taylor and the Benchley families, and deeply regret the hurt and loss my criminal actions caused them. I make a full, unreserved and sincere apology to the families of Sheriff Dave Ransford, Deputy Sheriff Jim Crogan, sheepherder John Adams, ranchers Tim McGee and Alan Hanover, as well as the family of Miss Cadie McClements.

"I regret the assault on Deputy Carl Fuller, who can no longer work as deputy, and the hardship this has caused his family and make a full and unreserved apology. I am deeply sorry for all my actions and the crimes I wrought upon the communities of Albany County and Laramie County, Wyoming, and Lincoln County

Nebraska, and Denver City, Colorado. I wish to make amends in that the entirety of my monies and savings and investments and properties are to be divided fairly amongst all those people so mentioned. So be it."

With emotions already high from the full confessions and detailed allocutions of both men, the Cheyenne community gathered here in court is affected yet again by the shaking, stuttering Donnelly. This time, instead of anger and outrage, Faraday senses sadness – and those mentioned are only some of the souls Donnelly has tormented.

"The prisoner may resume his seat."

Sturrock motions to the pasty-white Donnelly to sit down and he does as he's told.

"What say you, Mr Faraday?"

"I am satisfied, Your Honor, that Mr Donnelly's apology and reparations meet the People's requirements."

"Very well. All interested parties please be advised to make application for compensation at their earliest convenience through Mr Donnelly's attorneys, who are under a court order to dispense such compensation fairly and in a timely manner. Now, Mr Buchanan, your client may make his apology and statement of reparations."

"Yes, Your Honor."

Bodecker refuses to stand.

"Mr Bodecker, you must stand up when you address this court," the Judge insists. "Do so at once."

"Your Honor, at this point my client finds it difficult to stand."

"He will get to his feet even if you have to hold him upright, Mr Buchanan."

As Bodecker struggles to his feet, begrudging of Buchanan's help, Faraday studies the packed courtroom. Newspaper reporters occupy almost one quarter of it, including several court artists. The leaders of the miners' unions and other interest and protest groups are present, silent for once. Present, too, are the families and the people to whom Donnelly has apologized, most prominently, the Alliance. Also in attendance is the mayor, in a discreet back corner as far from the reporters as possible while maintaining close proximity to the doors; Faraday saw him steal in at the last possible moment. Meanwhile, Governor Warren awaits the news in his office, quite probably pacing the rug in front of his desk.

If Donnelly had been dreading his part, Bodecker looks bored and detached.

"Your Honor, may the court remind Mr Bodecker that his apology is expected to be wholly and utterly sincere. Lip service to the many people he has harmed will not do."

"Thank you, Mr Faraday. You are so reminded, Mr Bodecker," the Judge says.

Bodecker rolls his eyes. Obviously, it wasn't his idea to admit to his crimes and suffer public humiliation, and he is not about to go down looking like it was.

"I, Loren Bodecker, hereby offer my full and sincere apology to the people who have suffered as a result of my crimes…"

Buchanan forcefully hands him a sheet of paper. Bodecker takes it and reads, his tone flat. "As head of a once large and prosperous empire that has now failed due to my greed and ambition, I have caused catastrophic loss and suffering to a great many people by my criminal actions. For the hardship of all involved, I now offer my sincere regrets and unreserved apology."

Bodecker returns the paper to Buchanan who gives Judge Callaghan a hopeful look – he is satisfied with his client's efforts, so why wouldn't His Honor be…

"That's all you have to say, Mr Bodecker?" the Judge checks. "No compensation, no reparations?"

"Your Honor, any interested party who wants to sue for damages can contact Mr Bodecker's legal firm in Denver. At this time it is not certain what remains of Mr Bodecker's assets."

"I see, Mr Buchanan. He *does* understand that he is required to part with them?"

"Yes, Your Honor, he knows."

"And that his legal firm is under a court order to dispense them in fairness and in a timely manner?"

"He does indeed know, Your Honor."

"If his legal firm and financial people try to pussyfoot around, they'll have me to answer to, among others."

Pussyfoot?

Language like that means the Judge means business.

"There will be no pussyfooting, Your Honor," Buchanan says.

The public gallery chortles in spite of the grim tension.

"So, Mr Faraday, do the People view this apology as satisfying the conditions of the plea bargain?"

"No, Your Honor."

"Your Honor…" Buchanan protests.

"How so, Mr Faraday?"

"Since Mr Bodecker has satisfactorily allocuted to the planning of the murderous attack on the Alliance families, I would expect him to apologize directly to the Keaton, Taylor and Benchley families. Mr Bodecker managed to be a silent partner to murder and treachery throughout this terrifying ordeal, I think it about time he spoke with earnest feeling. Unless he does so, he has not satisfied the terms of the plea bargain."

Buchanan turns to his client. "My client agreed to the terms, Your Honor."

"Go ahead, Mr Bodecker. Sincerity is required by the People."

Bodecker doesn't move.

"Your Honor, Mr Bodecker managed to confess his crimes. There should be no problem apologizing for them."

Someone calls out from the back of the courtroom. "Give the great lump a prod!"

The Judge thumps a warning with his gavel. However, no one dares to respond to the heckler and give them away. The Judge peers around the courtroom looking for the perpetrator. All is still so he continues.

"Have your client proceed as instructed, Mr Buchanan."

Buchanan hands over the sheet of paper once more and whispers furiously in Bodecker's ear.

Bodecker snatches the paper. "I offer my sincere and unreserved apologies to the Keaton, Taylor and Benchley families for my criminal acts against them and regret the shocking and grievous harm I have caused."

The paper is tossed onto the table and he sits down.

"No, Your Honor, it won't do…"

"Your Honor, my client is only capable of so much."

"So what you are saying, Mr Buchanan, is that your client's callous *in*ability to apologize is equal to his callous *ability* to commit crimes?"

Buchanan smooths the hair on the back of his head; his expression is pained to say the least. "You could say that, Your Honor."

"Is the court expected to shift its expectations that low?"

Faraday lets that one ring while he turns to John and Amy Keaton seated along with the others in the first row of the gallery.

Time to put an end to all this for good.

"Your Honor?"

"Yes, Mr Faraday, what light can you shed?"

"Only this. I would beg the indulgence of the court and ask that John Keaton be permitted to address Mr Bodecker and Mr Donnelly directly."

Murmurs fly around the courtroom.

John's eyes go wide with surprise, but the glimmer of light within reveals he is keen for such a chance.

Excellent.

Faraday turns back to the Judge.

"The court would be pleased to hear from Mr Keaton. Please stand, sir, to make your statement for the court. Mr Buchanan, Mr Sturrock, have your clients stand and face Mr Keaton. Get it done."

John clears his throat. "Thank you, Your Honor, for this chance."

"Proceed."

Remarkably, John faces the heinous pair and gets them to look back at him. Apart from surprise, one couldn't begin to imagine what they are thinking, but their expressions reveal more feeling than during their read-aloud statements. Whatever else transpires from here on, Faraday believes he has the satisfaction of the People.

John begins. "My daughter and my son were my family. You had them killed. They stood up to you. They weren't afraid of you. That helps me bear my excruciating loss every day. And I'd be glad if you don't hang, so that if you go to prison forever you too will suffer excruciating loss, of your freedom and the selfish kind of life you're used to. My Kelley and Mart had their whole lives ahead of them, they were good and smart and kind. Nothing can replace them. I miss them so much sometimes I can't get out of bed in the mornings like I used to. It's a struggle to feel the same about things I used to be right keen about. I have to hide my grief from my wife because I don't want to add to hers. She is their mother; her babies are gone and you took them from her. We pretend we don't feel it by keeping real busy with other things; by caring for our friends in their time of need. And there's been a lot of need because of all the evil things you've done. All the Alliance families have suffered because of you, and many other families besides. If you can't be sorry in your heart of hearts, then at least look for forgiveness from God. I figure the stain of your evil ways won't be gone any time soon; we will know it all our lives; my little baby grandson will never know his father. I hope and pray that all the people affected by what you've done can find some kind of healing. God have mercy on you, because the rest of us, even as God-fearing people, have exhausted all of ours. I reckon that's all. Thank you, Your Honor, for letting me speak."

John takes his seat. And a breath.

Bodecker and Donnelly appear bemused; no one would ever have dared to talk to them like that in the past, and now in front of everyone? Perhaps the novelty cut through.

From John's final remark Faraday gleans how very nearly the pair came to facing the noose; it was a close run thing after all! He's still pondering it when the Judge clears his throat to continue.

"You are welcome, Mr Keaton; the court thanks you for speaking so eloquently. And now, Mr Faraday, what say you?"

"Mr Bodecker will make his statement of apology mentioning proper compensation again, if it so pleases the court, Your Honor."

"Mr Buchanan, in order to satisfy the People, have your client reread his statement."

Bodecker makes a considerably better fist of it this time; gone is the arrogance and the callous disregard; there is no pathetic show of inappropriate defiance.

"Your Honor, the People are satisfied."

The Judge nods. "Very well. We will recess for fifteen minutes before I pass sentence. Court is adjourned till then. However, I remind everyone here present most strongly that no one is allowed to leave the courtroom. So don't go asking to use the privy."

"All rise."

And when the Judge has taken himself from the courtroom through the back door, everyone sits down again and remains eerily quiet, including the black suits and their clients. Faraday takes his seat next to Josh, who raises his eyebrows in a speculative fashion, but says nothing. Faraday pours water from the pitcher on his table into the glass tumbler in front of him. A check of Buchanan; he appears circumspect, fingering the corner of Bodecker's apology until it dog ears.

Faraday consults his watch.

Then, from the back door, appears McArdle, the Judge's clerk. He speaks to Buchanan and Sturrock, and then comes over to Faraday. The Judge wants to see them in his chambers.

Judge Callaghan's chambers

"Gentlemen," Judge Callaghan greets them. "In a few minutes we will be done with this trial. This town has never seen the like before and hopefully never will again. That crowd outside in the street, they are quiet for now but..."

"Emotions *are* running high, Judge, but I am optimistic their faith in our system of justice runs deep," Faraday interrupts.

The Judge coughs. "I cherish such optimism, Mr Faraday."

"Judge, we want further assurances our clients will be properly protected," says Sturrock. "Most of that mob outside wants our clients to hang. Now their safety has been compromised, how can we be certain they won't be shot dead on the way back to the lockup? Someone saw the means to get the result they want when they set that fire and now it has the potential to deliver a sentence beyond what you intend. A death sentence..."

"I appreciate your concern for your clients, gentlemen. However, the fire is a mystery I hope will be solved and dealt with in good time. Meanwhile, Mr Ryan has all those prison guards and every deputy he can lay his hands on, Mr Sturrock. Unless there are more of those mavericks taking aim from rooftops, no law-abiding person would attempt to harm your clients. The courtroom is locked down and no person or reporter has been allowed to leave. No one outside this courtroom knows what has transpired. We agreed to this arrangement. Are you now telling me you wish to make a motion to delay sentencing until after the repairs have been made? Speak up, gentlemen!"

Buchanan keeps his poker-face; likely the attorney is at a point where his concern for Bodecker amounts to a hill of beans and who could blame him. Sturrock, meanwhile, sighs away the remains of his disquiet.

The truth is no one wants this trial to go for one more day, let alone the time it might take to repair the burnt out corridor leading to the jail cells. In any case, as the Judge pointed out in their morning discussion on the matter, who is to say the vandal won't strike again, causing further delays or creating more danger?

Everyone agreed. The trial ends today.

Faraday clears his throat…

"You have something to add, Mr Faraday."

"No one wants a delay, Judge. If the judicial system can deliver this just outcome against the most powerful man in the territory, that it can be delivered without more violence, that Bodecker can be made to confess and unreservedly apologize, *and* make financial reparations, then we should be confident about our decision."

The Judge contemplates, over his spectacles of course. "And what say you, Mr Buchanan?"

Buchanan mumbles something he thinks the Judge would want to hear; Faraday is quite aware that the canny black suits have played the back end of the trial exactly the way they wanted.

Courtroom

"Mr Donnelly, please stand for sentencing."

"We are ready, Your Honor," Sturrock says while Donnelly labors to his feet, rattling his manacles and leg chains.

"Terrence Donnelly, you have been found guilty of the following: creating and organizing a group of hired guns called

'Maverick' for the purpose of committing murder; said organization is responsible for the murder of Sheriff Dave Ransford, Deputy Sheriff Jim Crogan, Miss Kelley Keaton of Bright River, the sheepherder John Adams, and ranchers Tim McGee and Alan Hanover of Albany County. You have been found guilty of the attempted murder of the Keaton family, Ben Taylor, the Benchley family & Sheriff Dave Ransford. You have been found guilty of the cruel and callous murder of Miss Cadie McClements. Guilty of the assault of the North Platte deputy Carl Fuller. Guilty of the abduction, concealment and deprivation of liberty of Luke Taylor; conspiring to murder Luke Taylor; and the attempted murder of Luke Taylor.

"These crimes have wreaked havoc and destruction upon innocent, hard-working people, who have gone to great lengths to protect themselves and their families and communities. Because of your heinous crimes this territory has lost two excellent lawmen. You murdered a young girl with your bare hands. I can't begin to imagine the workings of your mind. Your cruelty and wickedness have caused much suffering and affronted this community on a level I have not seen in all my years a judge. And now I pass the following sentence upon you.

"You are so ordered to be taken from this courtroom to live out the rest of your life in prison with hard labor and solitary confinement. You are *never* to be released. Nor know the company of decent folk again. And in suffering this heartless and cruel deprivation of liberty, while the ghosts of your many foul and dreadful crimes visit you daily, may God have mercy on your soul."

The gavel thunders.

Donnelly sinks back into his chair, but before he can make himself comfortable, the prison guards have grabbed him.

"No one is allowed to leave this courtroom while the prisoner is being removed to the lock up," the Judge announces; a distinct murmur ripples around the room.

Perhaps it is best that Emmaline is not here to witness this; of all the dangers Cliff has faced perhaps this is the worst, for despite the Judge's assurances, the fire has created a serious situation. The residue of kerosene discovered at the heart of the devastation indicates a deliberate act and likely one of ongoing criminal intent. Someone wants the prisoners exposed; there can be no other way of looking at it. Everyone in the courthouse has been on edge; investigation is proceeding with Mac at the helm, but public interest in the trial is vast and at this juncture finding the culprit amounts to the proverbial needle in a haystack. Or there is Cliff's perspective…

"This was an inside job, make no mistake."

Faraday is inclined to agree with him. But who?

Over their breakfast meeting, after they had discarded the idea of adjourning the trial until the damage could be repaired, a protocol was created for the prisoners' transfer between the jail cells and courtroom. This protocol was used to bring the defendants *into* the courtroom without incident. It is about to be enacted in reverse, with no public knowledge of what has transpired. Whoever has done this, whatever their motive, danger has now presented itself as a part of the trial.

Armed with his rifle, expression set and stony, Cliff escorts the guard surrounding Donnelly from the courtroom via the main entrance.

"We will wait until Sheriff Ryan returns," the Judge announces as the echoes of the party in the main hall sneak into the courtroom before the doors are closed by Bailiff Owens.

The exact moment the armed party has made it outside becomes clear, as shouts and protests from the crowd gathered in the streets beyond the courthouse erupt. Murmurs spin around the room, and then die, eerily, as they all listen. The Judge clears his throat, shuffles papers, asks his clerk McArdle to fetch him something, checks on the court reporter.

Some minutes later Cliff returns, calm and grim as ever, to resume his station. Even the Judge looks relieved.

McArdle hands the Judge some papers, and when these have been perused by the Judge and added to the pile in front of him, the Judge says, "Mr Bodecker, you will stand for sentencing."

Buchanan gets him to his feet.

"Loren Bodecker, you have been found guilty of conspiracy to commit murder; accessory to murder; attempted murder; conspiring the murderous attack on The Alliance; and murder for hire. Your empire, once considered a source of hope and prosperity for many citizens in this territory and beyond, became a murderous regime built upon your greed, ambition and cruelty. I have never known anything like it.

"We are a free people and we cannot allow evil men like you to assume power and control over what we hold sacred, most of all our lives and our liberty.

"You are hereby sentenced to imprisonment with hard labor for the rest of your life. You are *never* to be released. And would that these arrangements of deprivation and reflection ideally prove to be some kind of hell in a cage, then God have mercy on your soul."

The Judge slams his gavel.

"No one is allowed to remove themselves from the courtroom until the prisoner has been escorted to his cell."

Again, they all witness the prisoner beginning the long journey on the road of life imprisonment. Again, they are all silent, a silence disturbed a second time by the angry shouts and jeers of the crowd as Bodecker leaves the courthouse.

And then everything is shattered by a piercing scream.

Cliff

Cliff halts proceedings and hastily orders the guards and deputies to surround the prisoner. Then he stares down the middle-aged man who, from about ten feet away and standing behind the recently erected rope barrier, holds them all at the point of a rifle.

"Lower your weapon," Cliff orders him.

"He should hang!"

"How do you know he won't?"

"He got life, didn't he? Escaped the hangman's noose."

The crowd gasps as one.

"Somebody tell you that?"

"Somebody did, but I ain't no snitch."

"I see. What's your name?"

"Lang. Jeremy Lang. My son lost his job in one of Bodecker's mines. The mine closed. No other mines would take Bodecker employees. My son owed money to the bank for his house, the bank foreclosed, and my son couldn't take care of his family. He got sick, Ryan, real sick, and…and he shot himself." Lang begins to shake.

"I'm sorry for your loss, Lang, truly and deeply sorry."

"Bodecker goes to prison for life. What about my son's life?"

The crowd begins to press forward.

"Everyone move back – now!"

"We agree with Lang," someone shouts.

"Yes, Sheriff, we want to see him hang. Why are you protecting a murderer?"

"Because whether he hangs or not, it's my job as your sheriff to see him back to his cell alive. Now disperse, or I'll have you all arrested for obstructing justice. Mr Lang, put down your weapon now and I'll forget I ever saw you."

"I'll shoot all of you," Lang declares.

"Who will take care of your son's family then, Lang, when you hang at the end of a rope for killing me, or my deputies, or Bodecker. You want to hang for that? – because Bodecker won't ever hang – but you will if you kill someone in cold blood."

"That's just wrong," someone declares.

"You want law and order in this territory to make it a safer place for your families and your businesses. So why are you breaking it now? You've had your protest, and well and good, but if one of you takes one more step, or you, Lang, make one more threat, I will arrest you!"

Stunned silence…

One brave soul says, "He means it. Mr Ryan always means it."

Another says, "None of us wants to go to jail for that pile of crap…"

Cliff hopes a grin will help. "I trust you don't mean me, sir."

"No, Sheriff. Not you."

Some of the tension eases. Now to deal with Lang.

"Remove your weapon, Lang, or I'll remove it myself." He adjusts the aim of his rifle so that he can shoot Lang's Winchester free of his hand.

"C'mon, Jere, it ain't worth it," the man behind Lang says. "Sheriff's right. Wouldn't do your boy's memory no good."

"Lotta people fought long and hard, made terrible sacrifices, gave their lives, to get this justice, Mr Lang," Cliff says. "Listen to your friends."

"C'mon, Jere…" Lang's friend makes another attempt to get the man to back down, but Lang shrugs it off. He is too far gone and no amount of talking or cajoling is going to work. Grief and revenge have consumed him. His agonizing pain has turned into rage.

The crowd intuitively shuffles away from him. They want no part. Wise choice. In response, Cliff focusses his aim squarely on Lang's trigger finger. Another try, though, however many it takes…

"Lower your weapon, Lang, it'll all be over, and we can move on; I know people who can help you, but you need to lower your rifle."

Lang's trigger finger, unfortunately, has a mind of its own.

Their weapons fire within a split second of each other.

The explosions ring.

As do Lang's screams. His rifle lands in the dust. And he falls to his knees.

The crowd squeals and cowers, but stays put.

"I shot his hand, a flesh wound," Cliff shouts, his voice sounding raw to his own ears. "Get him to a doctor. Now everyone disperse! This is over."

He swings around to the prisoner escort.

"We're okay, Cliff," Clary reassures him, "all of us. Even Bodecker, more's the pity."

Pete's glance is flicking here and there, all over the place. "So where did Lang's bullet end up?"

"Get moving." Cliff waves them on.

Bodecker catches his eye. He barks, "Wait."

"Keep moving, Bodecker."

"You're bleeding."

"Gees, Cliff, you are…"

"You want justice that much, Mr Sheriff?" Bodecker sniggers.

"I don't want that grieving man to set one foot inside a jail because of you. Now get moving."

With Bodecker returned to his cell and the prison guards at their stations, Cliff admits that the searing wound in his side is beginning to overpower him.

He leaves the lockup behind and instead of returning to the courtroom, he steps into the dazzling light of his office. He opens his coat and touches the side of his gut. Blood oozes freely over his fingers. A mortal wound? Would you look at that…

He grins, grimaces… here he was thinking he would live to be an old man too old and cranky for Emma to want to know.

"Sorry, Emma," he whispers as a vision of her swims into view.

He can't think of anyone who deserved it less than him, considering whose life he just protected, and yet who should it be but him? It's what he does…

TWO

Be still, sad heart! and cease repining;
Behind the clouds is the sun still shining;
Thy fate is the common fate of all,
Into each life some rain must fall,
Some days must be dark and dreary.

Henry Wadsworth Longfellow
The Rainy Day

Aftermath

Amy's pacing is relentless. "John Keaton, do something!"

John looks up from his anguish. "What am I supposed to do?"

"That man! That stupid, stupid man."

"You shouldn't speak about Cliff that way…"

"Not him! Good grief, John Keaton, the one who shot him. Better that Bodecker had hanged than this happen to Cliff."

"Don't think he'd see it that way, Amy."

"Oh, I think he would! What is the good of any of it?"

"Amy…"

"No, John, we did this to him!"

John grips her shoulders; stills her. "No, we didn't. An angry, grief-stricken man with a rifle did it. Think, Amy! That man could've been us, but it wasn't. We could've done that, but we didn't. We didn't take the law into our own hands, we stuck by the law like we're supposed to. Like Mart would have wanted. We stood over his grave and swore it. Now, no more talk of blame."

He'd sent Tip for Father Nugent because Sara wouldn't let go of his hand; not even Ethan could pry her loose. And when the priest quickly arrived he looked pinched and pale and uncharacteristically distressed. He gazed down at Cliff, who lay motionless on the old Doc's surgical table, and gave a deep sigh. And he said, "You did right to send for me, Luke."

"He wasn't Catholic yet, Father."

"He dearly wanted to be. Nevertheless, he's a baptized child of God and that's good enough. Stay and pray with me, young man, if you have the courage for it. He would want it, of that I am sure."

"I'll help him," Sara said. "We'll stay, Father."

From out of his cassock pockets, Nugent produced a black prayer book and a small brass container. He seemed calmer then.

"In nomine Patris et Filii et Spiritus Sancti. Amen..."

Luke can't recall Sara holding his hand for this long since way back at his father's funeral. They returned to the house *that* morning and sat for hours and she held his hand; he felt lost and scared. He didn't know what he was supposed to do next, until Ethan came to him and said *we keep on going, one day to the next, and it'll get better, you'll see.*

He looks at Sara's sad eyes. "No one would've ever believed when Connors and Pa made that deal it would come to this."

"Nothing is ever consigned to history, Luke. Everything we do has consequences, even for the generation down the road. The past, present and future are infinitely connected, always. I see that now."

Red Sky would agree; would say exactly that if she were here. But at this point he's sure not even Red Sky could give him comfort. And, although in his own way and with gentle words of wisdom, Nugent had tried to give comfort, the struggle to feel it goes on.

"What are we going to do about it, Mr Faraday?"

"I don't know, Judge."

"You don't know. Isn't that dandy; you don't know!"

"Do you know, Judge?"

Judge Callaghan stops his pacing and surrenders a deep sigh.

Faraday feels his eyes sting. "This is my fault..."

The Judge folds his arms. "How d'you figure? No. No one is to blame. Besides, the bullet was meant for Bodecker, originally... that Lang feller can't be right in the head, shooting the Sheriff."

"Pete said as much. Judge, Cliff had been struggling of late."

"Had no bearing on it. He wasn't afraid of this case or the trial or anything to do with it, Mr Faraday. He was tested in fire, that one, and came out as pure gold." The Judge swallows hard. "But that young reporter leaving him, that rattled him."

The Judge's insightfulness catches Faraday by surprise, although it shouldn't. A gruff exterior often cloaked the man's compassion and his humanity; how could anyone execute the position of judge without a sensitive understanding of human nature. Faraday experiences a rush of gratitude.

Sadly, the Judge murmurs, "Bring Lang before me tomorrow morning. I want to talk with him."

"Yes, Judge."

With a heavy chest, Mac considers Cliff's white face. He takes up his limp hand and holds it tight.

"I'm so sorry, Cliff."

Wasn't supposed to be this way.

"Guess it's a blessin' Emmaline's not here, seein' you like this. I reckon you'd be feelin' that if you could. I talked to Clary and Pete; they said you tried your best to talk that Lang feller down. Wasn't nothin' else you could've done, apart from standin' clear and lettin' Bodecker get shot. Wish ya had, Cliff, I can't deny that. Why'd you have to go and be so goddam noble. If only that lyin', murderin' sonofabitch was layin' here and you were…

"Nope, I take it all back. Wish Emmaline *was* here. You were her hero and she was yours, and she'd know exactly what to do and say."

Luke

Caroline looks on Cliff with a gaze full of admiration. "I can't believe a man such as our Mr Ryan is lying there like this. When we first met, I had just arrived in Cheyenne; you, Luke, had been arrested by that dreadful sheriff in North Platte and the state I was in! Well! I'd woken *Sheriff Ryan*; his eyes were weary; I'd disturbed his dreams, his hard-earned rest. If only Emmaline were here, she could bring him back. He loves her so."

Luke knows all too dearly the significance of her statement, however whimsical it may sound to others. He folds his arms and leans against the doorjamb, wondering what Cliff would think of it, but with him in a coma this deep and deadly they may never know.

They'd had a reprieve; Cliff survived the surgery and now it's a waiting game, as the old Doc calls it. He'd sent Nugent word of it; word came back in a flash… *our hearts are made for hope, be steadfast!*

"Maybe. Maybe he doesn't see the point anymore."

"You didn't give up," she replies, "so why would he?"

"The point of Emmaline, I mean."

"Why do you say that?"

"Because Emmaline left him without hope."

"Are you sure?"

"About Emmaline and them ever being together, yes."

"Then you are saying his hope could come from somewhere else. He only has to remember where…"

"Caroline, he's unconscious for God's sake..."

"Do you know?"

"Know what exactly?"

"Where his hope could come from?"

He sighs. "I think so. I've a fair idea."

"Good. He has so much courage. He is not even afraid to die. But maybe he would like to see Emmaline again one day."

"It's been two days," he points out.

"He's not exactly Lazarus, is he? Anyway, all the more reason. Sounds like you could do with a dose of hope yourself. You've seen too much killing, Luke, and you stared your own death in the face before this very man pulled you back from the brink."

He observes the utter stillness of Cliff lying in coma; he looks mostly dead except *he's holding on*, the old Doc said, *clinging to I don't know what.*

"I can't be certain it would help him."

"So you're afraid to try? He needs your help and you know what that is."

"Caroline..."

"Even the Judge refuses to continue with the other trials until this situation is resolved. So help your friend resolve it. We can't stay like this forever."

"No. We can't. You're right."

"It's what *all* of us need."

This will be difficult for him, he's resigned to that, but there's nothing to lose and everything to gain. Mart would have done nothing less for him. And he has never forgotten what he felt in San Francisco: at the moment Mart died in the bloody snow, everything he was he charged Luke with being. Here is its purpose. He's tried so hard for so long. He's weary to his bones and sad and dark to depths he didn't know existed.

Sad, dark and weary ain't an excuse for not doing what you should; if you want to be alive you accept sad, dark and weary, that's the deal, otherwise be dead because only dead people don't feel, period. There it is, Ethan's voice; never far away and always ready to cut through. Ethan has never said this; Luke just knows he would be saying it if he were standing here.

Be steadfast!

Nugent's more positive take. A pick-me-up in the face of it.

All right. Challenge accepted.

As he crosses to Cliff's nightstand, Caroline continues to talk. "Nobody can see their way forward while the hero of our tale lies half way between life and death."

He picks up Cliff's bible. "Seems to me, Caroline, you read a lot more novels than you let on."

"Yes, I confess I do. Is that your idea?"

He nods, hoping she doesn't think him idiotic.

"You've must have read to him from every other book on those shelves over there. But for what it's worth, I believe that is the right one."

"I appreciate that, Caroline."

"I'll leave you to it then," she says as she moves towards the door. "Good luck."

Mart had one. Mart the preacher… he smiles at the memory.

Don't you ever read the Good Book?

Don't have to. Don't want to.

Never did no one harm to read it.

Says you. You gonna be a preacher when you're growed up?

Mart said no, he wasn't gonna be a preacher; but they were only eleven years old. Mart should've gone off to college and become that preacher; Luke never understood why he didn't.

Mart's dark end had dimmed some of the light he'd always shed on Luke's life; but there is still a little left to help him do this.

He opens the cover and finds an inscription there.

> *For James Ashcliff Ryan.*
> *Thank you for being my guard and my shield.*
> *God bless you. Always, Emma.*

Well, he won't read that out loud. That's likely to be a setback he doesn't want to get the blame for. Still, as his eyes wander over it for second and third time, he dearly wishes he had the answer: how can something so clearly meant to be go so wrong?

A question for another time and place.

There are all kinds of paper markers stuck in lots of places, hanging out the sides, poking out of the top, cover to cover. Very handy, considering he doesn't have a clue where to start. These spots obviously hold some particular meaning. Good enough.

He puts his fingers to the most prominent marker and opens up Cliff's Bible at the spot. The marker itself looks important, being a small card, cream colored, and printed back and front in fancy writing. Looks like a poem. The impressive heading reads:

ST PATRICK'S BREASTPLATE

Sure. Had to be. Nothing simple for their Cliff.

After a thorough reading, once to himself and then out loud for Cliff's sake, it becomes clear that this is a request for protection, a breastplate being old world armor and here used as a metaphor. How could he ever hope to fully understand it? One verse seems particularly appropriate for the moment. He reads it again out loud:

"...protect me today against every poison, against burning, against drowning, against *death-wound*, that I may receive my eternal reward..."

Mart would have appreciated this prayer; that moment in the forest, when his blood stained the snow deep red, was his last thought of heaven? Was he thinking of his *eternal reward*? Knowing Mart, the answer has to be *yes*. But how does this breastplate work if good men go down believing in it?

He returns the card to its position and considers the Good Book itself. As usual with all Bibles the print is small and close together, but handily Cliff has underlined a couple of nearby passages. While he gets his tongue set in his mouth for speaking words he never imagined he'd ever say, he gets a sense of doing something helpful.

And he reads, slowly: "I lift up my eyes toward the mountains; whence shall help come to me? My help is from the Lord, who made heaven and earth. May he not suffer your foot to slip; may he slumber not who guards you: indeed he neither slumbers nor sleeps, the guardian of Israel.

"The Lord is your guardian; the Lord is your shade; he is beside you at your right hand. The sun shall not harm you by day, nor the moon by night. The Lord will guard you from all evil; he will guard your life. The Lord will guard your coming and your going, both now and forever."

He looks up and smiles. "The part about the mountains reminds me of home. I used to look up at the mountains every day. I guess the only grand things in my existence. Or my possession." But that's all he understands. "Do you get this, Cliff? – because that bullet got you fair and square."

Then Amy walks in, carrying a white bowl of something strongly scented, what of exactly, or even vaguely, he couldn't say for the life of him. As long as it doesn't smell like the stuff she used on him not so long ago.

"Oh, you are a good lad."

"Thanks, but this is hard and I don't get it."

Amy plants her hand on his shoulder. "You will, I'm certain."

"Maybe a hint?"

"You are a contradiction, Luke. Wasn't it you who said you believed Kelley was finally free in heaven?"

He concedes the point.

"Faith. Hope. And love."

That's it? That's all she's got?

She pats his shoulder. "Why don't you keep reading? It'll do us all some good. I want to sponge Cliff with this solution."

"What is it?"

"A solution for all that ails you."

He grins. "Good answer."

"It's good to see you smile. Now, read. I want to hear what Cliff would like us to know."

An interesting thought.

He finds a marker of scrap paper in a chapter called Micah.

"Arise, present your plea before the mountains, and let the hills hear your voice! Hear, O mountains, the plea of the Lord, pay attention, O foundations of the earth! For the Lord has a plea against his people, and he enters into trial with Israel."

He's unsure what to think of this section, although the trial part is relevant. He flips back to where he first began, the place kept by St Patrick and his breastplate, and finds more underlined passages.

"Hear, O God, my cry; listen to my prayer. From the earth's end I call to thee as my heart grows faint."

And then in the next section, "Only in God be at rest, my soul, for from him comes my hope. He only is my rock and my salvation, my stronghold; I shall not be disturbed. With God is my safety and my glory, he is the rock of my strength; my refuge is in God."

He reads this twice more, his ponderous efforts in counterpoint to the trickle of solution through flannel and the rhythm of Amy's precise, caring movements. The effect is peaceful, and should be at odds with the life and death struggle going on inside Cliff. When he looks up he notices Amy's smile is unexpectedly content; he thinks her face is what peace looks like, such is her serenity.

Understanding comes to him. Flows into him.

So, death kills the body, but not the soul. And the soul is more important because it is intended for eternity.

Eternity. Now there's a notion.

"It's becoming clearer," he says, feeling enlightened, although unsure if he believes it with the same conviction as Cliff had recently come to believe it. He decides he will read aloud the *only in God be at rest, my soul, for from him comes my hope* passage every chance he gets and before he reads anything else. A prelude, Jennifer would call it. She had the right words for everything.

Amy finishes up what she's doing. "I thought it would."

The doctor enters, giving them both a start.

"How is he?"

"Peaceful, I think," Amy tells him.

A stethoscope is placed on Cliff's chest. "Heartbeat is steady."

"Steady good, or steady bad?" Luke asks.

"Just steady. And that's cause for hope, don't you think?"

"In this room," he says, "we are steadfast."

The old Doc gives a firm nod. "Good. Because hearts can be funny things. Strong one minute and broken the next. This heart here is deciding which it is. Hope he works it out soon."

He imagines Cliff's heart is high up on a mountain, trying to decide whether to commend his soul to life that knows no death, or come back down to earth and face whatever comes.

Luke

Thursday

Morning sees US marshal Dan Hummer, three deputies, four prisoner guards and about twenty troopers assigned from Fort D.A. Russell's 3rd Cavalry all fully prepared to escort Bodecker and Donnelly from the lockup, into a US Marshal prison wagon, down to the depot, and onto the train with a jail car, heading for the heavy security prison in Cañon City, Colorado.

The Alliance, meanwhile, has made a plan of its own to gather outside the jail gates, while Sara and Raina remain at Cliff's bedside...

Luke meets up with Ethan and Tip; the Severini boys and Signora are with them. They watch the blue-coated troopers and their impeccably groomed horses get into formation along both sides and the rear of the prison wagon; their captain looks on while the sergeant gives orders to the men.

John and Amy arrive, and Tressa, with Adam in her arms, all of them rugged up against the chill. Caroline, Ben and Uncle Richard, who had perked up considerably at the idea of seeing off the man who almost ruined him, are but a few minutes behind the Keatons.

They only speak to greet one another, nothing more.

The cavalcade sets out; it remains tight in formation yet spreads wide enough to fill almost the breadth of Ferguson Street, with Hummer, chomping on a fresh cigar, driving the wagon; he has one of his deputies sitting beside him and the other two riding point.

In the back of the wagon itself, two of the armed guards keep travel accommodations confined and uncompromising for the prisoners, while the other two guards ride on top of the wagon, their shotguns like metal chimneys. The cavalry supplies an undeserving sense of occasion to the proceedings, which although understandable, is unfortunate.

Luke takes no notice of the prisoners; he can't bear to look at them any longer. No matter what anyone says, no matter how hard his head aches at the thought (and it does ache), they should have hanged for what they did; in his mind they are already dead.

Once the cavalcade has fixed its rhythm, the Alliance forms a horizontal line, some of them linking arms, some holding hands. He, Tip and Ben are wearing their long coats, the ones Emmaline once described as *filling with air and throbbing like great birds of prey.* The Alliance is still in town, always strong, never bettered, and with fixed determination to see this to the end, they begin to walk.

This is their lap of victory; this is them damning those sonsofbitches to hell and casting them into the fire.

Let this be a sign to those who seek to destroy us.

They haven't gotten very far when the Captain, mounted on his gleaming dark bay, allows the procession to pass by him; he turns his horse, moves into the middle of the street and waits like a park statue until they are forced to stop and look up at him. They hold their straight line, exactly like they agreed when planning last night should anyone try and stop them.

"Mr Taylor," he calls out from his shiny saddle.

"You appear to know my name, Captain," Luke answers him.

"Captain Michael Anderson of the 3rd Cavalry, at your service." The man is likely thirty-something behind his horseshoe moustache. His blue coat drapes partly along the horse's back. White-gloved hands are easy on the reins; hat sitting low over his eyes. And that horse… Luke has rarely seen an animal as beautiful.

"Captain. Is something wrong?"

Anderson doesn't answer at once; instead, while a cold wind pulls on their clothes and whistles in their ears, he runs his gaze along their line as if inspecting his troops, that is, until it halts on Tressa, holding Adam, who starts squirming at the lack of action.

"As you can see, Captain, we are peaceful."

"Are you armed?"

"We are not."

Anderson abruptly lifts his gaze to meet Luke's once again. "Mind you keep your family well back, Mr Taylor."

"You'll have no trouble from us, Captain. You have our word." Besides, they got a lot of fresh horse manure to avoid on the long march to the depot. They intend to keep well back all right.

The Captain gives a terse nod, tips his hat and instead of urging that expensive piece of army horse flesh forward to join his troopers, he goes around their line and heads to the rear.

"Now what..." Ethan mumbles beside him and glances over his shoulder.

Luke looks for himself.

Captain Anderson turns his mount about twenty feet back and then sends Luke another stern nod.

"Son of a gun, he's gonna ride drag," Ethan declares softly.

"Let's go..." And when Luke starts off again, so do they all.

The prisoner transfer wasn't publicized, so folks have stopped whatever they were doing in utter surprise to watch what is quite the spectacle, even from behind. Cheyenne loves it when the troopers come into town; maybe folks are wondering where the band is. When they cross 17th Street and then 16th Street, deep into the busy part of town, street traffic is forced to move aside. People begin to clamber to see, confined as they are to the sidewalks by the presence of Captain Anderson's troopers, yet compelled to follow this peculiar procession to its conclusion: the depot and the train bound for what they hope will be Bodecker and Donnelly's very own piece of hell on earth.

A man yells out from the sidewalk as they pass, "That's right, Taylor, you kick those damn bastards outa town!" His voice sounds raw and... "Tell Cliff Ryan to get back on his feet real soon!" ...swallowed up by emotion.

Luke gulps back his feelings, too. And then he shuts out all the commotion on the sidewalk. Keeps his eyes forward. Hears only the horses, and the wheels of the wagon, and the boot-crunch of his family as they march.

After a day of dodging reporters and trying to keep low at Cliff's house, evening comes down at last, and Amy and Signora Severini bring food.

"You eat, no?" Signora says, frowning and smiling at the same time, and pinching his cheek.

"I'll eat," he says.

Amy sponges Cliff yet again with the scented solution. "You see, Rosa, how I do this."

"Si," Signora replies and then she breaks into Italiano at the rate of a stampede; Luke marvels at how Amy understands a word.

"That's right," she says, "it draws out the poisons, invigorates his heart…"

"Cuore grande, eh?" Signora replies as she crosses her hands on her chest, her shiny doe eyes gazing down on Cliff.

Luke grins and thinks she's referring to the size of Cliff's heart.

"So," Amy says, "are you planning to sleep in a bed tonight? – preferably your own?"

"Who me?"

"Of course you. Who else would I be talking to? You've spent the last three nights in that chair. Someone else can stay here tonight."

He shakes his head. Truth is, he wouldn't be any other place. How could he be?

"I know you miss her," Amy says softly.

"I'm fine," he punches out.

"Mm… I'll send John around about ten to check on you."

"If Ethan doesn't beat him to it."

She sighs at Cliff. "We owe him so much."

"Si, molto," Signora murmurs. "Buona notte, bambino."

"She wouldn't call Cliff bambino, would she?" he whispers as Signora leaves the room.

Amy grins. "I don't believe she would."

Then the doctor ambles in. "Evenin' all. How's the patient?"

"You tell us," Luke says.

"Mrs Keaton, that solution astounds me; I can smell it all the way from the front door of this big old house. I remember when the house came up for sale. My wife wanted it and then we heard this new deputy bought it. My good lady said, how is it possible that a deputy can afford a house like that? Turned out he was a young lawyer from Chicago. And here he is. Mm, his color's better. Let me near now." Out comes the stethoscope followed by a thorough examination. The old Doc lifts the covers and checks the bandage. "Good."

"How is he?" Luke asks.

"He's fighting. I mean, he was always strong, but now his heart rate is up. His pulse is stronger. And, as I said, his color is better. His extremities are warm. His lungs are clear, good breath sounds. The wound is clean. This is nursing care at its best, and I think we have the best right here."

Luke gives Amy a smile; she's blushing.

"We sure do, Doc."

"Let's hope he makes an appearance soon, hmm? See you tomorrow. Let me know if you need me."

"I'll see you out, Doctor."

"Thank you, Mrs Keaton." As they walk out, Luke can hear the old Doc saying, "That boy of Ethan's will be in bed next..."

"Luke? Don't you worry about him."

"He's been through a great deal."

"I've got my eye on him. And so has Ethan..."

It's inescapable.

Eventually, the house is quiet again.

"You missed an interesting day," he says by way of beginning their evening conversation. "This morning I met Captain Anderson from the fort. Knowing you, you're already acquainted with him. He was impressive. And I think he liked the look of my cousin. Well, she is special. I worry about her, Cliff. What's she gonna do with her life now, besides raise Adam. She's young. She can stir the heart of an army captain. Good for her, I hear you say. Yep. You gotta know you're alive, right? So, what will it be tonight..."

He decides to check out the bookcase in the living room, now that the one in the bedroom no longer inspires him. He lights a lamp and runs his finger along the middle shelf, guiding his vision across the spines of Cliff's books. He comes across an unusual one.

There's no title on the spine, which makes it intriguing.

Curious, he removes the volume, and places the lamp on the lamp table nearby. He smoothes his hand over the book; it seems old and yet barely used.

He opens the cover. Dark and flowing script fills the page. An inscription. He moves closer to the light and reads it.

To my grandson, James Ashcliff Alejandro Alvarez Ryan, if you should be blessed to meet a woman for whom books are worth more than gold, words more valuable than money, the persuasive truth of passionate writing more stimulating than wine, then let this book be a symbol of all that you love in her and of how much you love her. If she would be the woman who would value this book more than gold and money and wine as symbol of your love for her, offer it to her. If she would accept it, then I know you are in excellent hands. Your loving Grandmother Juanita Alvarez. 18th August 1874. Live your life to make the dreams of the world come true.

His eyes sting and fill with moisture.

Emmaline! Again, how can something so right go so wrong?

So what is this mystery book? He turns the page and gulps.

Emma. A Novel. By the Author of Pride & Prejudice.

He has goosebumps.

Kinda takes his breath away.

Of course, no one could be married to Jennifer and not know this author is her favorite, Jane Austen. And he recalls her distress when Dermot burned her collection of Jane Austen novels. If only to feel her close to him, he needs to read some of it, no matter what it's like. He takes it back to Cliff's bedside.

"Don't get mad. We're reading *Emma*. Reckon we could both use a dose of this Jane Austen right about now."

He decides to read *only in God be at rest my soul* later on before they sleep; instead, he wipes his face on his shirtsleeve and begins. *"Chapter One. Emma Woodhouse, handsome, clever, and rich, with a comfortable house and happy disposition, seemed to unite some of the best blessings of existence; and had lived nearly twenty-one years in the world with very little to distress or vex her."* He stops and looks up. "Not too bad. Keep going?"

Ethan

Sara stirs honey into her tea with enough noise to spook cattle. "I'm worried about him, Ethan."

He grunts in reply. His newspaper needs reading.

"I know he's missing her, but he refuses to speak to me about it. He looks thin and tired."

"He's worried about Cliff."

"Yes, but he's missing *her*."

"Okay, he's missing her, what else is there to say?"

"Talking would help, wouldn't it?"

"Why?"

"I don't know, it just does."

"For you maybe. Not for Luke."

"And then there's the... the...."

"Quartz ore?" Ethan suggests and then regrets his sarcasm.

"What are we going to do about that?"

He shrugs. "It ain't going nowhere."

"Ethan," she sighs in frustration.

"Sara," he says, sitting forward and finally giving her his full attention. "When Cliff wakes up, the trials will continue and then they'll finish and then we go home and then we work out what to do about the quartz ore."

She groans. "I don't like this open-ended living. There never seems to be a conclusion to anything."

He understands. Gives her a smile to let her know. "None of us do, but we're trying to make the best of it."

But she looks away. "And what if Cliff doesn't wake up?"

"He will."

"You are always so sure of everything."

"And you wish you were more like me."

She sighs. "Where would she be now?"

He frowns. "Who? Jennifer?"

"Mm."

"You'd know that better than me. She probably went to St Louis to talk to her brother first. His name is Frank, a good man, if you're wondering. Sara, you changed your mind about her..."

"I can see that he loves her with all his heart, but I don't much like to see it breaking..."

"Aw, it ain't breaking. The reason she's so good for him is because she stretches him."

"I tell you his heart is breaking."

"Nope. He's being stretched. Just don't know it. He'll work it out. Now if the worst happens to Cliff, that would break his heart."

"You think you know so much, Ethan Benchley."

"I know the boy."

"Oh, for heaven's sake."

"When Cliff wakes up, you will see the end in sight, I promise you. Drink your tea."

Cliff

The light in his office is oddly bright. Blood, on his side, warm, running out of him, dripping through his fingers; he is falling; falling and falling without Emma's arms to catch him. The floor looms up before his eyes; he anticipates with dread the pain of...

Impact... his eyes are thrown open.

With alarming force, his bloodied side leaps into agony.

The pain, searing pain, helps him locate his memory.

He's been shot. The Winchester.

Bodecker. Where's Bodecker? Donnelly?

The lockup. He just left it, and they are securely behind bars.

He decides to get himself off the floor. Find Mac. And the old Doc. All about him the air is thick with a strange smell; the light now is gray, like that before dawn... except for the tinge of yellow coming from somewhere close by. Is he dead? Where are the angels? He didn't make it to heaven? Wait up. This looks like his bedroom. And he's not on the floor. He's in bed and there is a pillow behind his head. He makes a better attempt at moving, but the pain in his side tortures him into submission. He lets out a yelp of some kind. At least he's found his voice. Gingerly, he swivels his head to the right. Is anyone there? Asleep in the chair, with the Bible open text side down on his chest, is Luke.

Utterly confused, he lies very still for a long time, watching Luke's chest rise and fall beneath his Bible, while *only in God be at rest, my soul, for from him comes my hope* keeps playing over and over in his head. Then, bewildered but calm, he carefully takes his hand away from his wound; his cupped palm is filled with blood. He staggers to a chair, but he's falling. Someone is calling his name. He puts the blood into their hands. And then… he's lying here in bed.

All right, he can't have died and gone to heaven because Luke's there. Really there. The thought pulls a grin. He draws a deep breath. His wounded gut objects. He's alive!

Only in God be at rest, my soul…

Why do people always appear younger when they are asleep? Luke looks like a boy.

"Luke."

A twitch.

"Luke. Damn it, wake up."

His Bible begins to slide as Luke stirs.

"And watch my Bible."

"Huh?" Luke catches the Bible and sits blinking in the dim light. "Cliff?"

"Sure. Who else?"

"Cliff," he says again, sitting up, closing the Bible and carefully placing it on the nightstand. "Thank God…"

"What happened?"

"You lost a lot of blood."

"I…yes… blood."

"But the old Doc thinks you're gonna be all right."

"You could look happy to see me."

Luke grins at him. "Thirsty?"

"Yes," he says, relief breaking like a wave inside him.

He watches Luke get up and cross the room. He hears the water being poured into a glass. "Bodecker…"

"Gone. Donnelly. Gone. Cañon City yesterday. On the train. With Dan Hummer, his deputies and prison guards. There was a military escort from the fort as well."

"Gone…" he murmurs.

"It had a certain flair, I guess…"

Good old flippant Luke, hiding a barrel of emotions. Or maybe he's past caring. Who could blame him?

"That's that then," Cliff says, unsure whether his ambivalence about not being there is a good or a bad thing. "What is that smell?"

"Amy."

"Amy? Where?"

"No," Luke chuckles as he's bringing him the water. "Amy's concoction."

"Oh. Not that stuff that makes your eyes sting?"

"No. Not that one."

He drinks till he's breathless. It's good; something earthly about drinking, about needing to drink; he's alive; God didn't want him yet. He changes the direction of his thoughts. Luke seems to know how to hold his head and give him the water.

"This seems familiar."

"Mm… the boot's on the other foot."

"Who'd have thought… Luke, my books, all over the place… what the…?"

"We've been reading." Luke eases himself back into his chair.

"We have? And my good chair – looks like you made a nest."

"Reckon I have. Kinda cozy. How do you feel?"

"I don't know. Tired…"

"Go back to sleep."

"What did we read?"

"Most everything, I reckon. You were out of it a long time."

"My Bible?"

"You seemed to like it."

Luke's voice begins to sound distant.

"And sometimes we read…"

What was that? Jane Austen… *Emma.*

Emma. Emma. Emma….

Emma.

He jerks awake. "Emma…"

"Lie still, young feller."

The old Doc.

"I believe you are going to be all right. You need a lot of rest. And I mean it."

Cliff looks around, feeling a little frantic.

"Easy, easy now... I cauterized the wound, stitched you up. You've been unconscious since Monday afternoon. It is now Friday morning. So, you need food and rest."

"Damage?"

"You won't be wearing that smart gray suit again."

"Doc?"

"Blood loss. You didn't damage anything vital. Bullet nicked your liver..."

"That's not good."

"...but I got that sorted out. Not bad for an old coot like me."

"Thanks, Doc," he breathes. "I owe you."

"You don't owe me a thing."

"Mm, don't forget to send me the bill then."

The old Doc chuckles. "Hungry?"

"Maybe. What's on the menu?"

"Amy Keaton's chicken broth, I believe. My Lord, that woman can cook. Saw that Italian Signora assisting in the kitchen. Think she might have put some of that garlic those continentals are so fond of into the soup. Amy Keaton says it can fight infection. I've yet to find fault with anything that woman has to tell me."

Cliff swallows. Licks his lips.

The old Doc has the water close by and helps him drink.

"When can I sit up?"

"In a moment. Let me look at your wound first."

An inspection follows.

"Tender, I know. But it looks like it should. When you sit up, you have to take it easy. You're still healing, and there are stitches. You break them, you bleed. I may have to operate again."

The old Doc's diatribe about his wound is making him queasy, and he's thinking twice about sitting up when Luke saunters in with Amy in his wake holding a tray with a steaming bowl on top.

The old Doc seems pleased. "Precisely what the doctor ordered," he jokes. "Come on, Mr Taylor, let's have the good sheriff a little more upright."

Is he still sheriff? Didn't the mayor declare him incapacitated yet; promote Mac permanently?

He catches Luke's eye. "Do I start charging you rent?"

"Very funny. Relax and let Doc and me sit you up."

The old Doc chuckles. "Keep forgetting you're married to a doctor."

When it's done, and the giddiness subsides, Amy Keaton moves in with her bowl of chicken broth.

"Thank you," he says to her, with all the sincerity he can muster.

Her dark gray eyes sparkle at him. "You're welcome. Now open your mouth."

"It's hot… too hot."

"Blow on it," Luke says.

"Do you have to be here?"

"Good, good," the old Doc croons, "things seem to be going along splendidly. I'll come back this afternoon. But fetch me if there's a problem. Goodbye all. See myself out."

The old Doc departs.

He goes cross-eyed staring at the steaming spoonful of broth before his eyes.

Luke comes to his rescue. "I'll do this, Amy. You have enough hungry mouths to feed."

Amy lowers the spoon into the bowl. "Are you sure?"

"No doubt in my mind. I got this."

"If you're sure," she says, handing over the broth. "I'll see to things in the kitchen and return later."

"Really, you've gone to enough bother…" Cliff chimes in.

"It's no bother. Goodbye, Mr Ryan."

Her teasing robs him of a reply. He watches her sachet out of the room.

"She…" he says and stops.

"Don't know how John puts up with it."

Cliff grins.

"This looks good," Luke says. "Even I could probably attempt some."

Luke slowly feeds him the broth. And it's very good.

"You have a letter from Lamont, by the way. It's in that pile of stuff over by the window."

"What is all that?"

"Get well wishes from the entire population of Cheyenne."

He frowns and swallows the next spoonful.

"Chase Deloight sent a telegram wishing you a speedy recovery and to let you know that Lamont is a model prisoner."

"Eva."

"What was she like anyhow?"

"Not our type."

Luke chuckles and rests the spoon. "*Our* type?"

"Don't start."

"I won't. Still, I get the idea – uncomplicated, undemanding and happiest in the kitchen."

"Something like that," he grunts because laughing is out of the question.

"Yeah, we'd hate that." Luke picks up the spoon. "One more."

"Sleep."

"Last one."

He obeys. And then slumps. "Tell Signora, *grazie* for the garlic."

When he wakes sometime later, everything is clearer to him; he doesn't feel physically stronger, but more anchored in this earthly existence. It doesn't mean his every thought is without Emma; he still hasn't mastered how to do that, but he will. He has crossed a bridge; he's standing on the new shore looking back at his old life in which Emma had a part. But that opposite shore cannot be returned to, ever; it will be missed, and sadness will linger, but on this side is the future, there is no Emma here and on this new ground he will teach himself to forget her. He will conquer this new land if it's the last thing he does. And on that note, he rouses Luke from his afternoon siesta.

"You seem perky. Amy's soup and Signora's garlic sure are somethin' else."

"My head feels clearer."

"Good for you. Can I get you anything?"

"Those piles over by the window. I'd like to read them."

Luke's glance slips sideways across the room to the mountain of letters and cards. "A few maybe..." And when his glance returns, he's frowning. "What's going on with you?"

"I'm back in the land of the living."

"And it can wait a few more days till you catch up to it."

"Maybe," he concedes. "But what I have to tell you about me can't wait any longer. Only Cam knows, and Charlie Quaid for business reasons."

"Not Emmaline?"

He shakes his head. Emma will never know now. "No."

"You have a secret? About you?"

"Yes, but while I think of it, I don't want Emma knowing that I got shot and almost died. No one is to tell her, not Jennifer or you or Tressa, not anyone, got it?"

Luke's expression turns solicitous, almost fatherly. "Why?"

"For lots of reasons, you can probably guess most of them. Promise me, all of you."

"All right. But she might read about it somewhere, in a paper."

"I doubt it. And could you tell Quaid I'd like to see him?"

"Sure. What are you thinking, Cliff?"

"This is a new day. A fresh start. For me. I can't waste it."

"It's a gift all right. Now, what's this secret of yours?"

"I should've told you before this… I tried a few times, the last time being when you got ill after you had to give testimony about what happened in Porterfield's basement. You were recovering, I was working up to it and you told me to drop it."

Luke leans forward in his chair, resting his forearms on his knees. "I'm listenin' now, Cliff."

Luke

All the next day and throughout Sunday, Luke deals with scores of well-wishers who come to Cliff's door. He takes their cards and flowers, treats and good wishes, but on the old Doc's orders he admits only a select few for five minutes at a time.

And of those few, some bring words of appreciation and encouragement: Judge Callaghan, the Mayor and Governor Warren. Some bring humor and distraction from pain: the Alliance family in various combinations. Some bring tidings: Charlie Quaid, with newspapers to read; their conversation must've been downright interesting because when Quaid came out, he looked frustrated and could barely mutter goodbye. Cliff, on the other hand, looked as pleased with himself as a man could look.

And some bring spiritual ministrations, as Cliff calls it, namely Father Nugent, after whose visit Cliff is circumspect.

"He told me with everything that's happened and with Easter getting closer by the day, I probably won't be ready in time."

"So what? You'll be ready the week after, or the week after that."

"No. It has to be Easter. Luke, talk to Nugent for me. Get the lessons. And find Ruth O'Brien. And since you're so good with a Bible, you can help too. You might as well be useful…"

"Good? Er, I read the bits you underlined."

"I know. I've seen the dog-eared pages. You like mountains, don't you?"

"They remind me of home," he replies, unsettled. "I don't dog-ear pages…"

"Well, I certainly don't."

"Because Emmaline gave it to you?"

"So you saw the inscription."

"I'm nosey."

"That goes without saying."

"Sorry about the dog-ears."

Cliff takes a breath. "There are numerous books in the house from my time with Emma."

"Listen, Cliff, the other inscription, and the one inside *Emma*…"

"God, you *are* nosey."

"…and this notion about giving up on her…"

"We agreed not to discuss it."

"Since when? You just won't talk about her. And I can hardly argue with a sick man. You could have a relapse and then I'll get into trouble."

"Luke, seriously, I need this Easter. I've needed it since the day she left. I set my sights on it. I can do the work. Ruth O'Brien is supposed to help. I've been neglecting her…"

"Neglecting her? Cliff…"

"Tell Nugent…" The debate wearies him. "… and don't let him put you off."

Nugent stirs his coffee. "He's pushing himself. Why can't he take it easy just this once? Ruth is a good girl. She's going great. He shouldn't be worrying about her. And you're not Catholic."

"But he wants it. And I'm gonna make sure he gets it."

"Oh, that's that then, is it?"

"It is. He's hurt."

"I know he's hurt."

"No, Emmaline hurt him. Really hurt him. He needs Easter. It's been keeping him going."

Nugent rubs his chin. "He told you this?"

"If only he could've said goodbye on his terms."

"That certainly would've helped," Nugent says with a grim chuckle. "Ah, women… There's no end to their complexity. God love 'em."

And that, coming from a priest…

"Father, would you reconsider, for Cliff's sake, to help him recover? He wants a fresh start. A new way forward."

"I see where you're coming from, lad. How about we give it a trial? See how he goes."

Meantime, there is another debate going on – about the plea bargain. The papers are strangely quiet; Cam saved Bodecker from the hangman's noose, so the Bugle is reluctant to criticize him; the Tribune has mostly always supported Cam, so it doesn't have much to say either. For once, they report only what happened, leaving their appetite for emotion-charged editorializing to a far more vocal and discontented group: the public.

And so the debate over the plea bargain rages in the streets, as does the wisdom of Bodecker and Donnelly's exposure to the mob as a result of the fire. Almost everyone seems to feel the agony of it in some way or another. Not least because of their affection for their heroic sheriff.

While folks recognize Cliff's bravery for defending justice and demonstrating for them its significance – however daft they thought him for risking his life for Bodecker – they are not so kind to Cam. He already carried a heavy personal burden because of Cliff; now he copped some fierce criticism. He doesn't make excuses though, he merely shoulders more censure, and is honest with everyone: he made the correct decision, and Cliff had agreed with it – would he even be in this predicament if he hadn't?

Eventually, as the news spreads that Cliff will recover, relief replaces indignation, his improving health like a balm for raw nerves, frayed tempers and troubled hearts.

Cam and Mac, meanwhile, arrive at Cliff's house with some 'extraordinary news'. Luke thinks he ought to leave them to their visit, but Cam insists he stay.

"You need to hear this, Luke." Then he turns to Cliff. "Your suspicion about the whole thing being an inside job was correct."

"It's McArdle, isn't it?" Cliff says.

Luke can't believe his ears.

"When did you work out it was him?" Mac asks.

"Lying here, last night."

"And your deductions?" Cam asks.

"I used to think he was this irritating…"

"Pissant."

"Sure, Mac, thanks… who didn't have a clue how to be an appropriate clerk for the Judge. Even you pointed out, Cam, that McArdle couldn't ever be bothered to assist the Judge with something as simple as remembering his spectacles before going into court and he should be dismissed for it."

"Go on…"

"And then the fire happened. Everyone seemed distressed because of it except him. He came to tell me Martha had steaks for me in the Judge's chambers. I thought that was weird even for him. You were there, Mac…"

"Sure. I asked him if he were tryin' to tell us the Judge had called a meetin'."

"As if the morning wasn't strange enough."

"Only the beginning," Mac quips. "We were too darn busy to notice him after that, but I wish we had."

"I noticed he used his privilege of release from the locked courtroom to go outside."

"The Judge asked him to fetch something," Cam recalls.

"Yes, but he was outside when I escorted the armed guard and Donnelly to the jail after sentencing."

"He has admitted he did go outside with the express purpose of letting the crowd know the sentence. I don't know if you noticed or not, but he returned to court after you, Cliff, bringing the papers the Judge asked him to fetch."

A person could hardly blame Cliff for looking angry, although the emotion on his face dies pretty quick as if it has exhausted him.

Cam puts his hand on Cliff's shoulder; it seems to lend some comfort. "McArdle confessed. Judge Callaghan sentenced him to ten years in the Wyoming Territorial Prison in Laramie for inciting a crowd occasioning attempted manslaughter and obstruction of justice. The Judge found it very difficult."

Luke is having a hard time himself coming to grips with what he's hearing. Cliff nearly died because some stupid clerk made sure Jeremy Lang got an opportunity to shoot Bodecker?

"Sorry to interrupt," he says, "but why would he do this?"

Cliff manages a sloping grin. "Good question."

"And he started the fire?"

Cam looks his way, removing his hand from Cliff's shoulder after a firm pat of encouragement. "Yes, he confessed to that also, and the Judge gave him three years for it, to be served concurrently. McArdle said he got wind of a plea bargain, circulated a rumor that the sentences would be life with hard labor, set the fire to ensure the prisoners would have to be transferred by the outside path and then indicated to the crowd, after Cliff had transferred Donnelly and before he came back into court, that they would not hang."

"But how did he hear about the plea bargain before you?"

"He overheard Buchanan and Sturrock talking the day before."

"Sneaky pissant that he is," Mac mutters.

"He admitted to following me as I spoke to the Alliance, to the Governor and to you and Jennifer and he put two and two together. He left nothing to chance, however, and set fire to the prisoner holding room and the transfer corridor. Being at the scene of the fire, he was able to douse some of the flames and then discern when to call Pioneer Hook and Ladder to come and extinguish the rest before any further risk to the courthouse. Oh, yes, he is a wily character. This brings us to your first question, Luke – why."

"I think I might know," Cliff says. "Tell me if I'm wrong, Cam, but McArdle's father worked for Bodecker here in Cheyenne. He lost his job... No wait, all of you, before you say anything, I think McArdle's father beat his mother, regularly. And when he lost his job, he beat her so hard she died."

"The devil you say," Cam exclaims under his breath. "He only admitted to revenge for his father losing his job as his motivation. That when he learned there was a chance Bodecker could escape the hangman, he couldn't allow it to happen. It seemed extreme but with what you're saying it makes more sense. When did he tell you about his mother?"

"When Ethan and I got back from Bright River with the deed to the Diamond-T. He said he could see I didn't look too happy with life and that whatever was bothering me it couldn't be as bad as your father beating your mother to death over losing a job..."

Cliff has to stop and swallow hard.

"Perhaps this can wait…"

"No, Cam, I'm fine. When I asked him who or what he was referring to, and would he like me to get involved, he snapped at me that it happened to someone he once knew and took off. But I'm sure now this was his mother."

"Didn't even know McArdle had a mother," Mac muttered.

"He never spoke of his family."

Luke gulps down a surge of emotion. Poor, lonely woman. No one knew she even existed, let alone that she'd died in such a way.

"What kinda family is that," Mac adds after the moment stretches.

"One we can be grateful we don't come from," Cam says, so quietly that Luke almost whispers *Amen*.

Luke

Another trial is about to begin. Namely, Porterfield's. And with it those memories Luke dreads most. He steels his mind in readiness, determined not to lapse this time.

And come Thursday morning, he finds Cliff out of bed and struggling to dress himself.

"What are you doing?"

"What does it look like?"

"Then where d'you think you're going?"

"Courthouse. Where else?" His fingers tremble on his shirt buttons. "You need me. Don't deny it. You think I'd let you go into court alone to give testimony about what Porterfield did to you?"

"I don't need you to."

"Bullshit," he says, gingerly tucking his shirt into his pants.

"I don't want you to. Your testimony can wait another day at least. Get back into bed."

Cliff stops to catch his breath. "You know, Luke, the good thing about being a single sheriff in this town is that I don't have anyone who can order me to do anything. I'm responsible to the Constitution and to the folks of Laramie County who elected me and I don't see any of them objecting. Hand me my coat? Is it cold out?"

"It's fresh. Look, it ain't that simple once Amy Keaton's been feeding and nursing you…"

"Oh, no, don't start that. No woman, however charming, is going to order me back to bed."

"I'm fetching the old Doc."

"The old Doc likes his patients up and about. Luke, I'm only going to the courthouse and back. You wouldn't let *me* treat *you* like an invalid." His face maybe pale but there's nothing insipid about that look of determination. "Cranky bastard, you were. And the crankier you got the more colorful your language."

Sometimes you can't argue with the truth.

Cliff's arrival at the courthouse has a sense of celebrity about it; his return has everyone excited, except for Cam, who looks set to explode from concern, but at the last moment manages to hold it in.

"So," he says, his mouth in a tight line, "who wants to go first?"

"Luke can, makes sense," Cliff says, looking around him like this is the tonic he needed. "Good to be back. Listen, Cam, what's the jury like? Anything more on Porterfield?"

Cam ignores him and walks away.

Not long after, Luke gets on the stand and tells his dark tales of Porterfield. It's nauseating, but at least the jury listens attentively and looks sympathetic, which is probably the reason Andy Marks, Porterfield's defense attorney, declines to cross-examine him and Porterfield looks like a shriveled up prune behind those spectacles.

When Cliff takes to the witness stand, however, Porterfield's wincing grimace can be heard across the courtroom.

It draws the Judge's gaze momentarily. "Is your client ill, Mr Marks?"

"I don't believe so, Your Honor."

Luke has to hide a grin.

That's what unadulterated fear sounds like.

"Proceed with Mr Ryan's testimony, Mr Faraday."

"Thank you, Your Honor."

Cliff delivers his testimony. The photographs and the medical evidence are brought out and shown to the jury. Luke glimpses one or two of the men staring at him as the pictures get passed around.

Andy Marks takes up his cross-examination, debating Cliff's right to shoot the photographs. Even has the gall to suggest that the house in the pictures could be anyone's, and Cliff could have set it up. But Cliff remains resolute throughout the cross. The charcoal shadows beneath his eyes seem to deepen as the morning wears on.

Eventually, Marks has had enough of his own pointlessness. "No more questions for this witness, Your Honor."

Cliff steps down – gingerly. The Judge's frown is dark.

"Mr Faraday?"

"Your Honor, the People rest."

The Judge taps his gavel. "Mr Marks, you may present the case for the Defense after lunch. Court is adjourned."

When the courtroom is cleared, Luke helps Cliff to his feet. He's exhausted and pale. Cam tells him in no uncertain terms he's not to come back after lunch recess.

"Becoming a father has made you bossy, Cam."

"You're impossible," Cam sighs. "Anyway, you both did well. Marks' cross didn't appear to move the jury. Get some rest."

When he's gone, Cliff wants to go to Martha's for lunch.

"Home," Luke insists.

"Martha's."

Martha greets them with open arms. "What a sight for these sore old eyes. What can I get you, my handsome heroes?"

"Pie," Cliff says.

Martha gives him a curious look. "You sure?"

"I'm sure."

"And what about you, honey?"

"Pie sounds fine to me."

When it arrives, Cliff stares at it before closing his eyes for a long moment. Luke doesn't want to know what he's doing or why he's doing it, particularly if it's got to do with Emmaline.

Then Cliff opens his eyes and says, "I'm getting better."

"Sure, Cliff; never doubted it for a moment."

Considering his diet of broth and more broth, Cliff does well to eat half the generous slice of pie.

"Lunch recess is over," he says. "Let's go."

"Home."

"Luke, this is tiring."

"You're telling me," Luke says, annoyed. "Courthouse it is."

Amy and Signora ambush them on the steps. Amy's gray eyes remind him of thunderclouds.

"Told you so," he mumbles, trying to avoid Amy's glare.

"Amy, good of you to come," Cliff says, smiling. "Give me a hand, would you?" He puts his arm around her shoulders and steers her towards the courthouse doors. Her protests are gently ignored when she insists he go on home.

"Signora? You have something you want to say?"

"Si, si, Signore sceriffo. Casa!"

"Fra poco, Signora, *soon*," he says, enlisting little Signora as the prop for his other side.

"Adesso."

"Fra poco."

They sit each side of him in court, much to Cam's amusement, and Judge Callaghan's, who is about to swing his gavel to call for order when he spots Cliff between the two women. He clears his throat, looks down and gives that gavel of his a crisp smack.

"Mr Marks, you may begin your case."

"Thank you, Your Honor. I wish to call Dr Porterfield to the stand."

Louis Porterfield has obviously been told in the last little while that any man who needs two women to sit by him in court is not to be feared, because he takes the stand with lately acquired dignity.

Luke watches him through narrowed eyes. Memories of what he did are always close when Jennifer is far away. He listens to that twisted man declare under oath that Donnelly coerced him to do what he did. That Bodecker threatened him with all sorts of fearful things if he didn't comply.

"What fearful things, Doctor?" Marks inquires.

Luke closes his eyes. He can't bear to look at the rodent any longer.

"He threatened to kill me. He – Donnelly – said that Bodecker would kill me if I didn't comply."

Cam interrupts. "Your Honor, where is the proof that Mr Bodecker threatened Dr Porterfield?"

"Mr Marks?"

"I have a letter, dated October last year, Your Honor, from Mr Bodecker telling Dr Porterfield that he must comply with Mr Donnelly's instructions or face the consequences."

"What consequences, Your Honor?" Cam asks.

Porterfield says, "He would ruin my laboratory. Take it away from me. I have a son, back East…"

Luke opens one eye.

The Judge is frowning. "Is this true, Mr Marks?"

"Yes, Your Honor, Dr Porterfield has a son in Kansas City."

"My boy lives with his mother. Donnelly knows, knew… I had to do what he told me."

"Your Honor, this is the verified excerpt of the 1880 Federal census of Missouri showing the child's existence, then living in Kansas City, and a photograph of the boy with his mother."

Luke opens both eyes. Andy Marks is showing the jury.

"Your Honor, the defense places into evidence defense exhibit 10: the letter from Mr Bodecker to Dr Porterfield. And defense exhibits 11a and 11b: the Federal census excerpt and the child's photograph."

"Thank you, Mr Marks. Proceed with the witness."

"So, Dr Porterfield, Mr Donnelly threatened to hurt your son?"

"That's right. I had to do what he said."

"Was it your intention to kill Luke Taylor?"

"I kept him alive, I tell you. I kept him alive."

"No more questions."

"Your witness, Mr Faraday."

"Thank you, Your Honor. Dr Porterfield, was it Mr Donnelly's intention for Luke Taylor to die?"

"He… he expressed that intention, yes."

Luke's gut is telling him that maybe Martha's pie wasn't such a good idea.

"And you were to carry out that intention?"

"I was supposed to, but I didn't."

"I see. But you drugged him until he didn't know himself whether he was alive or dead, let him live in filth and degradation until he happened to be rescued."

"I… yes."

"But he wasn't supposed to be rescued, was he?"

"No."

"Luke Taylor would have died at your hands in those unspeakable conditions had Mr Ryan not come and rescued him."

"Objection. Conjecture…"

"Your Honor, Louis Porterfield has told the court he is a doctor of chemistry whose specialty is drugs of addiction; he would know accurately the limits of the human body in these conditions."

"Objection overruled."

"So, Dr Porterfield, Mr Taylor would have died at your hands in those conditions had Mr Ryan not come and rescued him."

"I kept him alive…"

"Really, Doctor? You didn't need to keep him in that condition, did you? You could have laid him in a clean bed, saw to his needs, feed him properly. But you starved him and degraded him. Were these Mr Donnelly's ideas, or your own?"

"I… I…"

"Speak up! Were these your ideas? Isn't it true that Mr Donnelly engaged you for this job because he knew exactly how you would treat Mr Taylor?"

"I…"

"He knew, because he had used you before to torture victims. Your methods were well-known and regarded by him. Isn't this all true, Doctor?"

"Objection. Mr Faraday is harassing my client…"

"Your Honor, if the Doctor would answer my questions…"

"Objection overruled. Dr Porterfield, you must answer Mr Faraday's questions."

Porterfield glances at the jury. "I had to do it. For my son."

"Your Honor…"

"Doctor Porterfield, answer Mr Faraday's questions."

"I am not a murderer."

"But you would have been, Doctor, if Mr Taylor wasn't rescued."

"I had to do as I was told."

"Dr Porterfield, in the front row behind me sits Mr Taylor. Look at him. He is here today because the man sitting nearby rescued him from your deadly clutches."

Everyone looks. It's unnerving. Porterfield's intense, beady expression, even without the syringe and the dishwater soup, gives him the creeps. Luke closes his eyes and retrieves the imprint of

Jennifer he made at the depot. Shining eyes, dainty freckles, dark chestnut hair, and deep pink lips that he longed to kiss from the moment his glance first fell upon them.

"Mr Donnelly didn't need to threaten you about your son, Doctor. The business you enjoyed because of Mr Bodecker's connections was all the incentive you needed to torture Mr Taylor until he was drug dependent, or dead, or both."

Silence. Luke opens his eyes again.

Porterfield is looking desperate, shaking his head.

"Isn't it true, Doctor, you are no longer with your son and his mother because of the business you undertook? They had to get out with their lives a long time ago, didn't they, Doctor?"

How does Cam know all this?

Luke glances sidelong at Cliff; he's surprised to find him watching him. And he shrugs, as if to say Cam wouldn't be doing his job if he *didn't* know.

"Doctor?"

"Yes," Porterfield admits in a low hiss. "But…"

"Where are your wife and son now, Doctor? The threat to their welfare has passed and yet they are not here to vouch for you, are they?"

"No…"

"You don't know where they are, do you, Doctor?"

"No."

"I doubt even Mr Donnelly knew of their whereabouts…"

"Objection…"

"No further questions, Your Honor."

"Mr Marks?"

"The defense rests, Your Honor."

"Very well. The witness will step down. There will be a ten minute recess and then I will hear closing arguments. Court is adjourned."

Cam delivers his closing arguments to the jury in a succinct, no nonsense style. No need for anything else, this tells them, because the facts, the evidence, the testimony and caliber of the witnesses need nothing more from him than sincere presentation. Marks, on the other hand, while also keeping his remarks brief, has nothing to recommend the innocence of his client.

It's not long before the Judge is saying, "Thank you, counselors. Gentlemen of the jury, you will now retire to consider your verdict in this case..." He gives them some instructions on what he expects of them before he declares, "Court is adjourned."

"All rise."

The Judge seems pleased to have a short trial on his hands.

Luke hadn't realized before but Amy's arm is curled around his. He tries to make sense of it... her eyes tell him. She was afraid for him, concerned for him; not only now, but then, back then. She has always been a good and loving friend to him. He wishes he could've done more for her; kept her babies alive. But this is all he can do now; procure all the justice he possibly can, no matter the cost, and not rest until it's done.

One hour later, the jury returns a guilty verdict.

The Judge addresses the panel: "Thank you, gentlemen of the jury, for your service and your attention to the details of this case. Your term of service has ended, however, I would ask you to remain while I impose sentence upon Mr Porterfield forthwith.

"Louis Porterfield, you have been found guilty of kidnapping, deprivation of liberty and holding a man against his will by the administration of addictive drugs; as well as attempted murder by the deliberate and willful maladministration of addictive drugs.

"The inhuman way in which you treated Mr Taylor turns the stomach of every decent person. And all the evidence has shown that he would have indeed died at your hands if he had not been rescued.

"Your part in the attempt to bring down the Alliance visited yet more horror upon this community, and drives home the depths of depravity to which all involved were prepared to descend.

"I do not find any mitigating circumstances in your story about your son and his mother, other than to factor into your incarceration that you actually have a son to whom you can be indebted for taking five years off your sentence.

"I hereby sentence you to twenty years in Wyoming Territorial Prison with hard labor. Court is adjourned."

❖

So as the days passed, as winter tried to lift and the sun became more determined, Cliff got stronger and his longed-for Easter was almost here.

People began to ease up on the self-pity and the bellyaching, and looked out for each other more. Cliff may have risked his life to do it, but his resolve to protect Bodecker made people think, at least for a while: revenge is not productive and justice brings peace.

Typically, Cliff bore no ill-will toward anyone, not even Jeremy Lang. And not Jeff McArdle.

In spite of all the turmoil, Cam found peace in his brand new daughter, Lily Margaret Faraday. And Meg pointed out *the future of Cheyenne and Wyoming had been secured; they were all safe again and Cam should be proud.*

His work wasn't over by any means. He moved quickly to indict Jeff McArdle's father for the murder of Annie McArdle, Jeff's mother; Oren McArdle was found guilty and given a life sentence. Judge Callaghan had made a decision, Cam confided, that anyone who committed a capital crime with a connection to Bodecker would not hang.

Annie McArdle's remains were located in her backyard and reinterred in the city cemetery, and she received a Christian burial. A great many flowers were laid on her grave. And as time went by it seemed as though the whole Territory's grievances were laid to rest there with her, the cost counted in whatever blooms or foliage could be acquired. Some folks laid barely a twig. The floral blanket became so wide the cemetery caretaker asked that folks put an end to it, but that request fell on deaf ears. Annie McArdle had gone from tragic obscurity to a household name, and her resting place a grave for a bruised and battered city to bury its tribulations and mourn its losses. The Mayor was quoted as saying: *Let them grieve.*

The trials of the rest of the empire culprits and misfits came and went. Cam cleaned out the county lock up and populated the territorial prison instead.

Marvin Tucker was tried for being an accessory to conspiracy to murder and found guilty. The Judge gave him seven years.

Raz Cole, having been found guilty of the attempted murder of the Keatons, received twenty years with hard labor. Jed Tyner, for the attempted murder of the Taylor and Benchley families, got fifteen years with hard labor, as no shot was fired.

And finally, Swinton Carter was pronounced guilty of the attempted murder of Emmaline, shooting an officer of the law – and murdering K. He was sentenced to life imprisonment with hard labor. Never to be released.

The days of the mavericks and their masters were gone forever, their deeds destined to rot in ignominy, if not in memory, for such deeds are never just consigned to history.

> The birthright we hold, shall never be sold,
> but sacred maintained to our graves,
> ...we will not be slaves. ~ Sons of Liberty

LT, April 1885

THREE

We had here... a view of Provincetown... under its shrubby sand-hills, with its harbor now full of vessels, whose masts mingled with the spires of its churches and gave it the appearance of a quite large seaport town.

Henry David Thoreau

Astonishing Chicago... she outgrows her prophecies faster than she can make them. She is always a novelty; for she is never the Chicago you saw when you passed through the last time.

Mark Twain

Provincetown

Tucked into the inside tip of Cape Cod

Provincetown is picturesque; no wonder the Pilgrims thought they should live here, that is until they realized Plymouth was more suitable. Indeed, with its topaz waters and bustling harbor, Provincetown is beautiful; full of color and character, ship masts and church spires, crowded waterfront and winding streets, sand dunes and beaches, rippling water in the bay and waves crashing with rhythmic reassurance on the seashore. And it's cold today, although due to the coastal humidity it's a different cold to Cheyenne's; unlike Emmaline, she has never had a problem with cold, it being as familiar to her as life itself.

But, in a long line of buts, the thing she hates – has always hated – is the whaling. As a small girl she would watch the whale carcasses being hauled off the ships and feel grief-stricken and disgusted. Even though Provincetown maintains a healthy whaling economy, since the advent of petroleum oil, and electricity replacing the need for whale oil, the industry is generally now in decline, which can only be good in her opinion. But Dermot is a man of the sea and he couldn't live without Provincetown, whether that meant nor'easters blowing the Cape to pieces and bloody whale carcasses, or a bounty of lobsters and bowls of clam chowder day after day.

This is his domain.

She and Frank pull up outside the house and stare at it.

Double-story, white-washed stone, slate roof, brick chimneys, 360 degree cupola, salt-hardy front garden, white picket fence.

Liberty Keep.

So much of their childhood had happened here.

Rumors came and went over the years that it was haunted; she would hear them from townsfolk from time to time. Yet in all the years she never encountered a single piece of evidence to support the claims; neither did Frank. And her brothers never mentioned anything either. As Duffy liked to say: you can't get a bigger load of codswallop, although she suspects Duffy only said that to protect her. *The Keep* was old; seafarers were notoriously superstitious; and as for the townsfolk... the more they had to gossip and tease her about, the better they liked it.

Ghosts or not, she wouldn't be at all surprised if the rooms still echoed with sound of her father's voice raised in anger, when before suppertime she had to present herself to him and give an account of how she spent her day. Always on edge but not wanting to appear so, one particular time she reported how much she enjoyed the whale carcasses to avoid his wrath, only to be told she was a liar, walloped on the back of her legs so hard she fell and sent to bed without supper. She was five years old. The next day she was too scared to report to him and put herself to bed without supper. Frank brought her food, read to her from her favorite book, and instructed her in exactly what to say next time, which they practiced, and with it being a resounding success the following day, she made it her unwavering formula ever after.

She gives a shiver and thinks she must have lost her mind to be doing this.

"Come on, George. Let's get it over with."

She takes Frank's hand and steps down from the cab. The driver spends some moments piling their luggage inside the front gate and then drives off. Meanwhile, they are still standing on the sidewalk.

"We haven't got very far, have we?"

"No." Frank's gaze flicks sideways. "But I think we're being watched."

Dermot spies their arrival from an upstairs window. He stays behind the curtain and watches them looking up at the house, free to study the daughter and wonder at the beauty that is so like her mother's. Since each day finds him seriously weaker than the one before, he is relieved she has finally come.

And Frank, too. Oh, yes. He knew Frank would come if the daughter did. But no grandchildren. He shakes his head, sadness seizing him. The last he saw of Frank's children was a girl as a baby. He remembers Conor and Patrick, but not the names of the girl and the two other females Frank and Jeanne had produced since they went to St Louis. And what would any of them know or care about him anyhow.

There is no one to blame; not even the daughter.

As they move up the path to the front door, the daughter mesmerizes him. She even moves like Aisling, with a gentle, graceful swing to her step. How could someone who had never known her mother be so much like her? The slow pace of his life nearing its end has given him pause to reflect. What has become of her since he disinherited her eight years ago? Who is she? She was always defiant and intractable. For now, her expression is unreadable, unlike Frank's, which is always open and agreeable.

"They're here," Felicity says from behind him.

"I can see that." He checks himself in the mirror, tells her he'll be down presently.

"Are you up for that?"

"I wouldn't say so if I weren't. Prepare some refreshments for them. They've come a long way."

"Of course, Mr Sullivan. Right away."

At the top of the stairs, Dermot takes a cleansing breath of the only type he can take – shallow. He listens to their voices, talking pleasantly to one another.

In the doorway of the sitting room he stops, and lets his eyes take in their presence in his house after such a long absence. Very quickly they see him. No one says anything right away. Frank seems a little overcome. The daughter is studying him closely. There is ice in her eyes.

"What are you staring at?" he says to her.

"From the urgent tone of the telegrams, I thought you would be bedridden."

"On the days Joseph wired I probably was."

Their lack of any kind of greeting doesn't bother either of them.

Frank comes to him and takes his hand in both of his young ones. "Father..."

Dermot studies him. "Frank. You look well. The family?"

"All fine, thank you. Jeanne sends you her best wishes."

"That's kind of her. Tell her thank you and give her mine."

"I will. Perhaps you'd better sit down."

"Before I fall down, you think."

"What's the matter with you, Father? Joseph wrote something about consumption – is that correct?"

"He speaks the truth."

The daughter clears her throat. "Tuberculosis of the lungs."

"Yes, it's fatal. I'm dying. Any day now. That's why I brought you here, to tell you. So what do you think so far?"

Frank's face pales and he sits down quickly. Poor Frank. After all, the drama is intended for the daughter.

"Don't know why we should expect consideration from you," she mumbles. Then, "Frank?"

"I'm all right, George."

Dermot takes the spot next to Frank on the sofa. "Sorry about that, Frank, my boy." Long time since he's been close to this good-hearted son.

"Who is caring for you?" the daughter asks.

"My housekeeper and nurse, Felicity Williams. Used to attend the physician in Boston every so often, but now I can't leave the house. The local doctor calls around. Joseph keeps an eye on me. Miles calls by from time to time. Now it's your turn."

"What would you like us to do?"

Dermot narrows his eyes on her. "What would you suggest?"

"I have no suggestions. I came because you asked to see me after all these years. If you expect anything more than basic pity, then you've wasted my time and yours."

"Pity at its most basic would be something at least."

"So you made us come all this way to impart the fact that you are dying. As far as that goes, you've always been dying. You've managed to combine death with living in every way possible, so don't think for one minute that your little announcement makes a scrap of difference to the rest of your life except for ending it. There are people who suffer worse than you every day, but they live their lives and find their way back if they fall behind. They don't sit around and mourn the dead while they punish the living. They go on. Unlike you. You're going to be very comfortable dying because you're used to it..."

"George..." Frank murmurs.

"Got that off your chest, did you?" Dermot grunts.

"I need to organize a telegram." And that said, she walks with her head high out of the room towards the kitchen.

Dermot scratches the back of his head. She's different to what he expected. She was right, of course. He is going to enjoy dying.

"So, Father," says Frank, rallying. "How long have you got?"

Dermot chuckles at him. "Not long at all. Thought I'd see how she turned out. What do you think?"

"George is George. Anyway, how does it matter what I think? If you want to know, it's up to you to find out."

Dermot grunts. "She doesn't make it easy."

"She came, didn't she?"

From the back upstairs balcony, she lets the soothing murmur from the seashore wash over her. Serenity travels across the peninsula with the onset of the chilled evening, and as daylight fades, the rhythm of the waves comes clearer, closer, a salty mist moving in with the night air. A sea gull releases its last lonely call for the day. She catches sight of it before it swoops away at will.

Frank and his father are talking quietly. She is half-listening. Frank knows how to get the best out of him; Dermot actually sounds normal as they carry on their conversation about his future, or lack of it. He's taken to bed. She's surprised he would go to the trouble of getting out of bed to greet them in the first place. He coughs often, and talks in short breathless sentences.

As she wanders back inside again, he barks, "Where have you been?"

"Outside." Where it's peaceful. She removes her woolen shawl.

"I can see that. But I thought you'd be interested in how I'm planning to die."

"Not particularly. When you're dead, Frank can tell me whether it all went to plan."

He stares at her, blankly. The thing about this sick Dermot is that he has none of the physical power or the strength of the Dermot she once knew. She would have to be a mouse to cower before him.

"You don't want to see me dead?"

"I remember thinking every day when I was young I would like you to be dead. But you were never one to make life easy."

He gulps and stifles a cough as best he can, white handkerchief to his mouth.

"I've seen quite a few people die," she continues. "Their bodies give up, but somewhere some part of them lives on, in their children, in the work they did, in the memories of their friends."

"They're the good ones," he prattles.

Frank sits back, smiling.

She closes her mouth and keeps it closed.

"Now what?"

She shakes her head.

He mumbles to himself. "Stubborn…" He points a shaky finger in her direction. "That's a ring on your finger. You married?"

The thought of this obnoxious man and Luke in the same room together collapses her stomach and gives her a chill.

"So?" she says, turning away to look at the series of framed watercolors on the wall. She always hated them, the whaling station pictures. Who would use amiable watercolors to depict such horror? Who'd want bloody, gruesome whale carcasses sitting on your wall? Dermot, that's who.

"Who is he?"

"You mean, why would he want to marry me?"

"Did I say that? Frank, did I say that?"

Frank shakes his head. "George, tell him about Luke..."

"Luke?" he squawks. "You married someone named Luke?"

She starts removing the watercolors from the wall. "I did."

"What are you doing?"

"If I have to be in here, I don't want to be looking at them."

"Put them back!"

She piles them up on the lamp table by the window.

"Come here and tell me about this Luke," he says crankily. "Where is he? Why isn't he here with you?"

"Because he carries a six-shooter and if he were here he would shoot you stone-cold dead. And we can't have you dying without the maximum amount of suffering, can we?"

The smile falls off Frank's face. Dermot's mouth drops open.

"Frank," he croaks, "you've met this husband?"

"Of course. We all attended their wedding. It was wonderful."

"What's he like?"

"He's young – strong – smart, and George's perfect match."

"Puts up with her smart mouth, does he?"

"He accords her a great deal of respect, in fact..."

"And her rude and stubborn ways?"

She aches with building tension; her muscles are twisting, her insides throbbing. And all the time, there's a voice in her head, chanting *you should have waited for him...*

Her eyes prickle and sting.

"He loves her very much," Frank is saying.

"Does he now? But not enough to come here and introduce himself..."

"Father, as George said, he has expressed the desire to shoot you. And he is a man of his word... generally."

"Is he now? Why does he want to shoot me?"

This is firmly directed at her. The trap! As if. Foolish man.

"He likes shooting people is all."

Dermot huffs, and chunters, "Very mature."

"George has a photograph from their wedding day in her luggage, don't you, George – why don't you fetch it?"

She glares at Frank. "It is not for showing."

But Dermot's gaze will not leave her face. "I would like to see you on your wedding day."

"Why?"

His eyes go dark with anger. "Fine. Don't show me."

He has the strength for anger? A long coughing fit follows, which answers her question. Felicity Williams comes in and tends to him. Jennifer watches closely as the woman carries out her nursing duties.

"Doing it right, is she, George?" Frank murmurs in her ear.

"Yes."

"Go and fetch the wedding photograph."

"No."

"And don't talk to him about Luke that way."

She lets out a sigh and fetches the photograph.

On her return, Dermot is recovered. She thrusts her cherished photograph in front of him and he takes it slowly and without comment.

He studies it for a very long time. "He doesn't look like a gunslinger. And still this man wants to shoot me, eh?"

She says nothing.

"He's young, like you said, Frank."

"One year older than George, almost to the day."

"Does he make you happy?"

"What do you think?"

"Can't tell, you're so grumpy."

"Whether you think so or not, I have a right to be happy."

"And Luke affirms that in every way," Frank says, smiling.

Dermot lowers the photograph. "So he's got spunk, has he?"

She nods.

"Frank," he says breathily, "there's a tin on the table over there. Bring it here."

While Frank is carrying out this request, Dermot puts her photograph on the pillow beside him. "He's not what I was expecting."

"I can't begin to imagine what your expectations would be and frankly I don't care."

The tin arrives; he puts it on his lap and fiddles with the lid.

When he gets it open, he pokes the contents with his finger. "Paper clippings. You sent me these, Frank."

"Yes, I recognize some."

"What are they?" she asks, curiosity getting the better of her.

"Oh, these… these are about you," Dermot says gleefully.

"What are you talking about?"

"Since you took so long to come, I got Frank to send me some things. Wanted to know what you'd been doing. Found out."

She has to sit down, taking the chair by the balcony door.

Dermot extracts a clipping. "You see, from a newspaper in that town where you live."

"Cheyenne."

"This one talks about Miles' friend…"

"*My* friend. Cam Faraday."

"And this one about your involvement with these courageous Alliance people. You caught an outlaw…" He starts chuckling. "I can well imagine that. I'm figuring that your husband might be one of these people."

"He is."

"Not a gunslinger. A man fighting for what he believes in." He lifts up a pile of clippings and lets them drop back into the tin. "Look at all these. I know more than you think. You've been in the thick of it."

She throws up her hands, gets to her feet. "I don't know what I'm doing here, I really don't…"

"I wanted to see how you turned out," Dermot says.

She blinks. Bastard. "Fine. This is me. I look like *her*. Satisfied? You can go on hating me for it, but you know something, I don't care…"

"George…"

"No, Frank. I left Luke to come here."

"You… you do look like your mother," Dermot says, pushing the tin to one side. "It was a cruel joke on her part to think she could be replaced by a copy."

She gasps. "The cruelty was never hers. And I certainly didn't kill her. You did. You got her pregnant. The blame is yours."

"George, I really…"

"No, son, let her talk," Dermot rattles. "So, it's my fault."

"Unless my mother had something else wrong with her, you made her with child and she died after she gave birth."

"To you!"

"Yes, I was the one. The luckless, wretched sap who ended up with you as their parent. Even now I ask *why me*? But who else should it have been? Why wish it on some other innocent soul?"

"Sap? What kind of word is that?"

"It describes me. That's what I am! "

He has no come back. He watches her with restless eyes.

"Did you love her?" she asks.

"What did you say?"

"I asked if you loved my mother? Or was her death purely an inconvenience that turned you into a…"

"George," Frank murmurs.

"You were the inconvenience," Dermot says.

"Thought so. The sap!"

"I loved your mother," he declares.

"Really? Capable of love, are you?"

He catches his breath.

Frank scratches the back of his head.

"Just because…" Dermot splutters and stops.

She finishes it for him. "… you didn't love me, doesn't mean you don't know how to love? Answer me this then. Did you love me while my mother was expecting me… did you anticipate my birth with joy… did you touch my mother's belly and consider what I might look like… did you even give a damn?"

Both father and son are purely shocked.

"*Well?*"

Dermot looks away. "Don't have to answer that."

"Can't do it, can you? Admit that once you had feelings for me… oh, you didn't know me, never dreamt of what I would be capable. If you loved my mother, and you wanted the child she was carrying, then you must have wanted me!"

"George, that's brilliant," Frank mutters.

Dermot looks defeated.

"Well?"

But he's not down for the count... "There's only one way you could have come to that conclusion."

She narrows her eyes on him.

"You're with child yourself. Aren't you?"

"What?" Frank chokes out.

"I asked you a question."

"Don't turn this around onto me!"

"Huh! Now who's avoiding the subject?"

"Is he right, George?"

"Oh, so right," Dermot barks. "She knows how her mother felt. Her mother loved her. I loved her mother. *Ergo*, I must have loved her! Simple deduction, but you have to know how to approach it."

"George, answer me."

She glares at Dermot. "Well? Is it true?"

"True, your mother loved you. True, I loved your mother. True..." He frowns and closes his eyes.

Fists clenched, she says, "Someone told me that if you and my mother and the boys all loved and wanted me while my mother carried me, then that would be enough love to make me into the woman I am today, a caring, compassionate one, in spite of your cruelty and... and what I endured."

"That's wonderful," Frank exclaims. "Luke told you that."

She nods. "He hasn't yet realized the extent of what you did, Frank; the love and care you showed me in place of this... man."

"What *you* endured?" Dermot declares. "What about what I endured? I lost her, for good."

"We all did, you selfish piece of work. And if Luke should lose me when I give birth to this precious child we both love so much, should he turn his back on *him*? Is that still your thinking?"

"George, you *are* with child," Frank breathes.

"He couldn't do that. Never. The child is a part of both of us. It's a miracle that life even begins. That love brings life into being is sacred. Luke loves this child, and you demanding I come here has divided us and hurt him. So I ask you again, and this time you must answer me or I will leave *now* and go back to my husband: did you love me when my mother carried me in her womb?"

Dermot looks down at his hands as if searching for an answer.

That word is, "Yes."

Felicity is arguing with Dermot, and losing.

"But you should not be out of bed. They will eat their supper and return. You eat your supper and they'll be back."

"I'll eat at the table with them and that's that! Get my robe."

So, in a short time, Dermot joins them at the table in the dining room as they wait for Felicity to serve their supper. Jennifer had offered to help and was given a flat *won't be necessary*.

Felicity, it seems, is a good cook as well as an efficient nurse. They eat clam chowder, vegetable salad and fresh bread. Dermot manages some of the chowder.

There is fruit on the table, arranged in a patterned porcelain bowl Jennifer recognizes from her childhood. She touches it, remembering...

"Have it," Dermot barks.

"Sorry," she says and whips her hand back onto her lap.

He gives an impatient sigh. "Have the bowl."

"I don't want it."

"Fine. Don't have it." And he starts coughing.

Felicity insists that he return to bed. Frank offers to lend a hand. Felicity declines the offer, but Dermot insists on Frank. Felicity follows closely, issuing instructions. Dermot, ignoring the poor woman, chatters to Frank all the way up the stairs.

Alone again, she stares at the bowl. The creamy glaze, delicate crimson flowers and leafy swirls. It had always beguiled her but she found out the hard way touching it was out of the question. It must have been special to her mother, she realizes now. She wonders if they would have liked similar things, such as the bowl...

Frank interrupts her reverie. "He wants to talk to you."

"The bowl... it was a favorite of hers, wasn't it?"

He pulls his mouth into a tight line, slides his hands into his pockets. "We knew this wasn't going to be easy. It's incredible what you've managed to do already." He sits sideways on the chair next to her and takes her hand in his.

"Frank, I need to warn you. Tuberculosis has been proven to be infectious. Felicity is an exemplary nurse, and to Dermot's credit, he always coughs into his handkerchief, but you need to practice careful hygiene while we're here and..."

"Wash my hands?" he finishes with a knowing smile.

"And don't get too close, if you don't need to, that is."

"Don't worry, I'm taking care. My sister is a doctor, isn't she?"

She nods, part in answer and part in relief.

Frank's smile widens. "George, I'm thrilled about the baby. You are going to be a wonderful mother. How do you feel?"

"I'm fine. I'm... happy. And excited."

"Of course you are. And Luke, how is he?"

"About the baby, thrilled. About me leaving him and coming here, very upset."

"But you said he has the trials to complete and other things..."

"Yes, but after all we've been through, we promised one another we wouldn't be apart. I broke the promise."

Frank pats her hand. "He'll get over it."

"I hope so. He puts up with my 'stubborn ways' because he is even more stubborn than I."

"I have faith in him. He loves you too much."

"Can you love someone too much?"

"George, you know I mean *too much* to stay away. Now go on upstairs. Go on..."

"Aren't you coming?"

"I'll be along."

The father of her brothers is upright against his pillows with his eyes closed. He looks extremely ill and old way beyond his years with those sunken cheeks and sallow skin. His forehead is always shiny, beaded with sweat. Each breath is an effort. His time is short; meanwhile the effort of receiving them and talking to them is taking its toll.

His eyes fly open, startling her. She holds her ground while they stare at one another across the room.

"You have something to say to me?"

"Sit down... please..."

As she moves to a chair, she notices the watercolors have been placed back on the wall.

"You're too far away... come closer."

She takes the chair near the bed.

"Better..." he grunts.

"Well?"

"You've already got what you came for... haven't you?"

"And what if I have?"

"The knowledge you now have... it doesn't change anything?"

"Not how I think about you, if that's what you mean." She clears her throat, looks at her hands. "You made your choices a long time ago."

"And now I have to live with them? Actually, I have to die with them."

Interesting, she thinks, and looks up again. He is watching her closely.

"But, Jennifer... I'm not going to die with all of them."

The shock of him calling her by her name – the *only* time in her memory – causes a momentary lapse in concentration.

"I sent for you so I could find out if asking you... to forgive me was worth it to me... and to you."

The wave of dizziness that strikes her has nothing to do with her pregnancy and everything to do with his last act of cruelty.

"Well?"

"You've got it wrong, haven't you?" she rallies. "I'm supposed to ask for your forgiveness for ruining your life."

"No, no..."

"Aren't I supposed to ask for it before you die so that I'll feel better?"

"No!" he barks and coughs. "You got what you came for. Now I want... what I wanted you to bring... with you."

"I don't love you. Whenever I tried, you were cruel. I loved Uncle Michael. He was a good man and he wanted to take me when I was a baby and raise me with love in a happy home the way my mother would have wanted, but you thwarted him in every way possible so you could take out your vicious anger on me."

"I know."

"You are despicable, but I'm supposed to give *you* peace of mind before you die?"

He drags breath into his lungs, alarming her. "I agree I have no right to ask much of you now. Tell me... the one thing... Luke most admires... and loves... about you."

"Don't drag Luke into this."

"Why do you protect him...from me, or... me from him?"

"That's ridiculous."

"You need this as much... as I do... how can I... face your mother?"

"I grew up never knowing my mother. How do you think that felt? And how do you think it felt being reminded constantly that I caused her death. How do you think that felt?"

"As bad as me... having to live without her."

"You're wrong," she shouts. "Worse. A hundred, a thousand times worse! Because you never loved me to compensate for what I lost. But your hatred for me compensated you. When you die and finally face my mother what are you going to say to her? I didn't care for Jennifer because she was a girl, a nuisance and not worth my time. I hated Jennifer because I didn't have the courage to face life without you."

Raggedly, he says, "Some of that is true... yes... but I'm hoping I'll say Jennifer forgave me... for being such a coward... and now she can live in peace. But I did give our daughter something, Aisling, I'll say... I gave her determination and a will to succeed... I did give you those things, Jennifer."

Turmoil rages within her.

"What do you say, Jennifer... You need this as much... as I do... for Luke's sake, too. I understand... he is angry with me out of love for you... I understand that... he is worthy of you... I drove you away and eventually you found... him. I see the hurt in you... being divided from him... hard to bear."

The hurt reaches into her bones; makes each breath an exercise in dreadful loneliness. Dermot can see that? Why shouldn't he? He has lived without his precious Aisling for twenty-six years.

"You...you know how it feels."

"Move along," she snaps.

"I need your compassion, Jennifer..."

"You've got some nerve."

He laughs with a cough. "Indeed, as I die... it's not for the faint-hearted... you and I are not that... never that... Jennifer, I need to leave by the right path... Only compassion... I know you can't love me. That would be impossible... but if God can want this pathetic man in heaven... surely you can want the same for His sake... if not for mine."

"God wants you? I should care what God wants? You never lost a case, did you? You were the supreme advocate."

"By heaven, you're tough. Made you that way, didn't I? I'm glad. We all say... how much you are like your mother... but you are like me, too... oh, yes... I wager... your toughness makes Luke feel safe. I know because... right now it's making me feel safe."

"What do you mean?"

"You won't say a cursory *I forgive you, father of my brothers,* and walk away. When you say it... you'll mean it and that means... everything to me."

"Stop it. You are pathetic. Just stop it."

"As you saw me as I was twenty six years ago... through the love you have for that child you are carrying... I see you through your young man's eyes... I was once a young man in love who breathed your mother's love... into my body every day... it kept me alive. In the picture... I see a man who loves you the same."

He stops and draws breath.

"Jennifer... forgive me... I can't die until you do... I am sorry for what I did to you... I was wrong and I was cruel... I've been hanging on all these weeks... waiting for you... to tell you."

"Why didn't you die weeks ago!"

"Listen to me... you were right... you were conceived out of love. Why didn't I love you... I was too grief-stricken to contemplate life without Aisling... I didn't accept her death... is my excuse... feeble and cowardly... I didn't realize what you were until it was too late... Aisling left part of herself behind... the best part... you... she wanted you to be a girl... said a daughter would be good for me... we didn't even...have a name for a boy... you were always going to be Jennifer... when she died... I turned my back on you..." He stops to labor through a series of shallow breaths.

Her mother, her beautiful mother who she never knew. So sad, so sad… "Mama." Her sorrow is so fathomless she has a vision of her own heart broken in two. Her body aches; tears flow out.

"I am so sorry you never knew her… she was extraordinary."

"It's too late for that."

"Yes… too late for all that now."

"And too late for me to know who I am. Half of me has been lost and I will never know that person… "

"You know who you are, Jennifer… got a better sense of it than most… including those who have their whole family…tree mapped out on a scroll in their attic. We have one… in the attic… will tell you everything you want to know… about your mother."

"It can't possibly do that."

"It could help…"

"I bet it doesn't have Jennifer on it!"

"Put it there… with Luke's name and all the children you're going to have… it's yours. I give it you… and I want you to have this house… *Liberty Keep*…"

"No! I don't want one single thing from you."

"You can bring all your brats here on summer holiday… Maybe when they're grown they'll want to come to Boston… study law or medicine or music… And then when it's time… you can leave it to them yourself… I want you and your angry husband to have it… Joseph has put it in my will… I've given you everything I have left… now grant me your forgiveness… please?"

She stares at him for a long time. Did the ugly, confusing, cruel upbringing he inflicted on her lead her in some way to Luke? She is not convinced that any child should have to go through *that* to find their true adult destiny; she considers herself one of the lucky ones in that regard. She was an abused child. In order to counteract the effects of her daily struggle to minimize the damage, she immersed herself in science and doctoring, and it often exhausted her.

But neither does finding Luke seem completely serendipitous. Circumstances in his life brought him to her. And yet, if it could be said that what Dermot did to her, however small in consequence, led her in some way to Luke…

"He healed me of the great hurt," she thinks out loud.

"How?"

"He gave me hope."

"Why do you speak... in past tense?"

She wipes her cheeks with her fingertips. "Because I left him."

"When I am gone... you will be right with him... we will make our peace... then his anger over me... the thing that parts you... will die with me."

She cannot deny this wisdom. Luke wants this man dead. He wants her free of him and the destructive misery he represents, and to love her and the tiny prospect in place of it. He wants her happiness, and with him there will be never-ending joy, enough to share with this broken-down man. After all, that's all Dermot really is. And with that thought she inhales a long breath and releases it.

"I forgive you."

For the first time in her memory, Dermot smiles at her. In that instant, she glimpses a resemblance to Frank; she almost smiles in return.

"Thank you, Jennifer... I am most grateful... I sincerely wish you a... lifetime of joy with Luke... you will have it... I feel it in these worn out bones... I will tell your mother... queen of the angels... we loved a daughter into being... and she can be proud."

❖

As their father battles on throughout the night, Frank insists that George go to bed. He sits with his father. Keeps his vigil.

How can he not recall the grueling years of their childhood, his and George's? Their abiding affection which existed alongside their father's willful torment. All the times Uncle Michael tried to wrest George away from their Father, hundreds of times, to give her the childhood she deserved. George only knew of a few incidences; he shielded her from the rest because to give her hope would have added to the cruelty she already endured. And so many times he wanted to tell her they were going to run away and start a new life, but that would have wasted their material opportunities and likely reduced them to a life of poverty or worse.

No, he decided very early that he would craft a life for her that in spite of her suffering she could still thrive. And it started when she was a baby and he a little boy; if she cried in her cradle, he would lift her out and tell stories, play, rock, walk and soothe her back to sleep. The nurse did all the dirty work; he kept all the joy, fun and affection for himself. George was a very good baby; and when she smiled up at him he received all the affirmation he needed. He missed his Mama terribly; his grief was assuaged by loving, and being loved by, the infant bundle she left in her place.

Why their father couldn't do the same mystified him for a very long time. Why wouldn't Father, who loved *him*, not love George?

In those growing years he did a lot of eavesdropping on Uncle and Father and their heated contests over George. And eventually he understood why Father was a man with two faces.

He was a tormented soul.

Nothing could help him.

While Uncle persisted with arguments, lawsuits and custody battles, Frank did deals with the devil, who was kind enough to his sons. He exploited this kindness to help George anyway he could.

They were forbidden from speaking about their mother, so Frank kept close his memories of her for as long as possible. They faded over time but have never left him. He adored her; she was his world. And then she was gone. She died with George asleep in the crook of her arm. He would never forget that, not ever.

All is long ago. Just memories. He has his own family of individuals who are busy making their own memories. And although he might not be the world's best father, he loves that tribe of rapscallions more than life itself. Each one is a gift. As George was a gift. His father taught him that; not because he was a good father to him, but because Frank had to find the father inside of himself to raise George, the last gift his mother ever gave him, the dearest and the best.

So, in spite of everything, his heart has room for gladness. He did his best. He has the life he wanted, and George, whose spirit was always too great for their father to grasp, is soaring to ever new heights. She, too, will have the life their mother wanted for her. Her capacity for whatever life throws at her constantly amazes him.

And this was most difficult of all her challenges…

Forgiving Dermot.

Luke's considerable worth doubles, triples, in his eyes. He has done everything right and Frank cannot fault him. Even to the point of arming Jennifer with the one weapon he never thought she would be able to use in her defense against Dermot – love.

In the early hours before daybreak he nods off in the chair.

After breakfast, it becomes clear that his father is close to death. In truth, he had been waiting for Jennifer, and now it was time. His breathing becomes even shallower than before and he wanders in and out of consciousness. The doctor from Provincetown attends him with Felicity's help.

Frank had Joseph and Miles summoned from Boston, knowing their father would hang on until they arrived to say goodbye. George sits sedately in the back of the room, having taken the whaling watercolors off the wall.

The poor man lies helplessly waiting to die.

And then he calls for George and she goes to his bedside. He only wants to hold her hand. They have never held hands.

George takes his sickly one in hers and says, "Don't be afraid."

Frank feels a sob in his throat, not on account of his father, but because of George's compassion.

"Aisling will come," he mutters.

"Yes. My mama. The queen of the angels."

"Yes… Aisling…"

This is the very last word he utters.

George retreats to the window and stands watch for Joseph and Miles. Frank remains at the bedside, observing his father's panting attempts at breathing, in such minute increments there can hardly be any life left…

George stiffens. "They're coming."

"Not a moment too soon," the doctor says. "He's nearly gone."

"They'll be up in a moment."

Frank goes to George and stands with her.

Joseph and Miles walk into the room with the local reverend. They nod a greeting and go straight to their father's side, murmuring final words to him. Then they stand at the end of the bed and stare at him while the minister attends him.

"How much longer?" Miles asks.

"Not long," the doctor says.

Frank goes to his side and sits down on the bed. "Father, it's me, Frank. I want to say goodbye. And God speed you on your way..."

She's returned to this old house... she drifts back and looks at her portrait. Did she once look like that? Flesh and blood! That was Dermot's Aisling.

And now in their bedroom.

Her sons!

Proud Joseph.

Incorrigible Miles.

Amiable Frank.

Tall, intelligent men gathered around Dermot's tired body.

And there, behold her baby daughter.

Jennifer!

That sweet, tenacious creature; her heart stamped with the imprint of the Creator: courage, compassion and kindness.

All is forgiven... it is time.

A new day is come.

Dermot... Dermot, it's time.

Aisling... you are exactly as I remember you... how I've longed to see you... never leave me again...

Come, Dermot! You've done what you had to do. Jennifer will be fine. She has Luke.

Yes, she has. As she was meant to. Now come!

Aisling... you will take me with you... God has forgiven me?

Come, Dermot. You will know all soon.

Can we be together now?
I watched you struggle, Dermot. Stop now and come with me.
This life is over at last? Stay with me...
Do not fear, Dermot. There is no fear from now on. That is over.
Stay with me, Aisling...
I will stay. Come!

"He's gone," the doctor pronounces.

Frank sighs.

It's over.

He doesn't feel sad; he's relieved.

But how must George be feeling?

He goes to her and stands beside her. He can't read her expression; but her hand finds his and squeezes firmly. She's all right. More than all right, he thinks.

For some time they are all silent except for the minister who is praying.

"You know, George," he whispers to her. "I had the strangest feeling."

George gives a fleeting smile. "Angel breath, Frank?"

"Mm..."

"You owe Ariel an apology."

"I think it was Aisling."

"Queen of the angels. Come for her beloved."

"Do you think so?"

"I don't know, Frank. It's what *you* believe that counts."

"I believe you gave Father his last chance at heaven, George."

She looks up at him, her gaze fixed and confident. "And I believe he gave me mine."

Luke

Yes, the days are passing, and while the calendar says its spring, winter struggles to lift. Jennifer has been gone three weeks. It feels longer. In all this time he has received one telegram, telling him she had arrived safely in Provincetown and she had met with Dermot. And it feels bleak. Without Jennifer he's unsettled, without the prospect of Evan the future seems lacking in promise. No matter what he does, or what other people do, he can't shake it off.

Weird headaches come and go. K becomes strong in his thoughts at such times and he realizes it will be a long time before his mind will be able to lay *everything* that's happened to rest. The terror is over, they are free of it at long last, but human memory is a delicate instrument and it's not about to stop playing its tune even through sheer force of will. It has to be convinced with endless perseverance that a person is no longer interested in listening to it.

So he decides to write more, and sketch more, (Jennifer always encourages him in these) hoping to reconcile his mind with the past by recording more of the present.

He's not one for precise times and dates of particular events; he likes storytelling better. Sometimes he writes in the first person, making it a personal account; but often he includes himself as one of his characters, third person and by name. With Jennifer he can discuss these kinda details; she enjoys it, and her eyes light up, and she tells him how much she loves his ideas.

Some folks might ask what he hopes to achieve: for one, use his creative abilities as a way to compensate for Jennifer's absence...

145

and leave something for posterity... follow his dreams, the ones Sara would prefer he didn't. All of these. He can't allow this battle to define him forever, so he sketches... and he writes...

Cliff's strength was returning quickly. It was plain for all to see he had embraced his 'fresh start'. That's what Easter meant to him.

Now, even though the Mayor had insisted he was to make a full recovery before he returned to his duties, Cliff did not sit around 'wasting time'; instead he spent at least an hour or two in the day with Father Nugent, as well as studying his catechism (as he called it). Cliff said he liked the priest's energy, and he learnt about parish life and what that meant to Catholics since it wasn't something he'd grown up with like most of Nugent's flock.

Miss O'Brien, meanwhile, considering what had happened to her, appeared to bloom before their very eyes. A lot of folks commented on what a fine young lady she was. One morning close to Easter as they were studying, when Cliff had to leave the room, she said to Luke that she still didn't know why Cliff had chosen her. Fact is, the workings of Cliff's mind were a mystery to a lot of people, but you knew that somehow, whatever he was up to, it would work out. Miss O'Brien answered her own question:

"Out of supreme Christian charity, I imagine. I'm glad he did, because in those moments of distress, when I think of my greatest failure, I remember what I've been called on to do and it lifts me up out of the pit and into the light again."

By the look on her face she probably didn't expect him to understand, but Luke knew about pits, very dark ones, as well as Cliff's ability to pull people out of them.

Eventually, Nugent gave them *all* permission, even Ethan, to attend the service where Cliff would get his final approval.

"Not approval, initiation," Cliff corrected him.

"Like joining a club." A club that cheered him up and speeded his recovery (the old Doc and Nugent both conceded that).

"I guess," Cliff shrugged.

"A club that won't let you eat meat on Fridays. That's fine. They all have their rules."

"Since when have you objected to eating fresh-caught fish?"

"It's not my club, and what if the fish ain't biting on Fridays?"

"They will be."

Cliff made what he called his First Confession on the Wednesday before Easter, a special event where he got to divulge all his sins and feel good about it. He said he'd already spent time preparing Nugent for it so his life wouldn't come as too much of a shock. Afterwards, when Luke admitted he couldn't see himself walking into a tiny wooden room and speaking randomly about his misdeeds, Cliff chuckled and described it like a visit to the dentist – you felt great when it was all over. Luke wasn't all that convinced.

And something else special came Cliff's way at eleven o'clock on Easter Saturday morning. Cliff didn't know it but the Mayor had arranged a little soiree in his office and invited a number of relevant guests to attend.

Luke walked with him down to the Mayor's office.

"What's this about?" Cliff asked him. "You know don't you?"

"How would I? You know I got the invitation same as you."

They arrived at the Mayor's and walked into his reception room with Cliff grumbling about how much he had left to do before the service. Dozens of eyes looked up and their accompanying voices went silent. The room was filled with guests, including: Governor Warren and his wife, Helen; Cam and Meg; all of the Alliance; a number of prominent Cheyenne businessmen; assorted county and territorial officers; acting sheriff Mac and his wife, Pat; deputies Clary and Pete; Judge Callaghan and his wife, Deborah; Father Nugent and several other people from his church that included Ruth O'Brien; Charlie Quaid from the Tribune; and Marshal Dan Hummer.

Cliff's grumbling died away. Applause replaced it.

Fortunately, Cliff did have a big heart, as Signora not long ago pointed out; a lesser heart might have given out from shock.

The Mayor came forward and shook Luke's hand, confirming the conspiratorial nature of his part. Luke stepped away, grinning, and stood by Ethan and Tip. When the Mayor drew Cliff forward into the middle of the room where everyone could see, their guest of honor looked like he wanted to feign a resurgence of his coma.

"Cliff, let me fill you in here," the Mayor said. "Several people came to me over the last couple of weeks, not the least being our illustrious governor, and our intrepid Mr Faraday, and said don't you think we should do something about Sheriff Ryan. Give the man a citation, or something."

Cliff rubbed that place on his forehead.

"So that's what we are doing today. Today we want to honor the man whose extraordinary efforts in bringing to justice Loren Bodecker and Terrence Donnelly and his so-called mavericks, and their ignominious cohorts, went far beyond his duty to his office as Sheriff of Laramie County and protector of this city. Cliff, on this citation I have here, the words read, and I didn't make these up – everyone here had a say in it – here goes:

"This meritorious service award and citation of honor is presented to Cliff Ryan, for his extraordinary courage, bravery, compassion, loyalty, cunning, skill and heroic sacrifice as Sheriff of Laramie County. A grateful community heartily commends him and salutes him with undying admiration and eternal appreciation. Cheyenne, Territory of Wyoming, April 24th, 1885."

Applause broke out then, louder than before.

The governor stepped forward, took the citation and after shaking Cliff's hand, presented him with it. Endorsed by the Mayor, the Governor, and the recently inaugurated President of the United States Grover Cleveland, the citation was smart, embossed with fancy gold lettering, and presented in a silver and ebony frame.

Cliff accepted it with his usual grace and aplomb, but mainly with astonishment. He was called upon to give a speech. That request nearly did bring on a relapse, but he pulled himself together, and thanked the mayor and the governor and everyone for the honor.

He thanked everyone for coming, for thinking of him and for taking care of him. He said he was glad to be alive and grateful for his many friends and colleagues. He said his job was a privilege and he felt proud to have served the community. And then he said, as much as it saddened him, it was time to move on, that it was time to be and do something else. And that he would never forget them, or this day and this honor.

"We half expected it," said the Mayor, shaking his hand. "You've taken your fair share of bullets..."

And heartache.

"I think it's more than fair. Good luck, Cliff. We're always here if you need us, for anything at all, even a chinwag. And we hope you don't sell your house and move away forever. Your contribution to this territory has been an unforgettable one."

No one reproached Cliff for announcing his resignation that day. In fact, it seemed entirely appropriate. He said if it hadn't been then it would have been on Monday morning. Dan Hummer said that with the endorsement from the President, Cliff only had to say the word and he'd be a fully-fledged US marshal. But Cliff's marshalling days were at an end, and Hummer removed his cigar from his white teeth and declared, "What a waste!"

Luke ensured that along the bottom of the citation, in gold letters, ran the words... *Live your life to make the dreams of the world come true.*

The next day, Easter Sunday, Cliff became a Catholic.

Nugent allowed them all to watch, seated in the back of the church, not understanding any or much of it, and some of them regretting its length. The church was full to overflowing with people. Everything inside it gleamed and the perfume of lilies filled the air. Beautiful, harmonized choir singing sent shivers down Luke's spine and a deep resounding organ thundered from the loft above all the way into his chest, reverberating around his heart.

Ethan leant across and said, "You'd think that Nugent could talk American."

Cam looked amused and winked. Ethan rolled his eyes.

At least Nugent gave his sermon in American. He spoke about the feelings of Mary Magdalene as she arrived at Jesus' tomb to find him gone, and an angel sitting there. This fear and uncertainty eventually became joy as she discovered her beloved Jesus was alive.

"For those of us who walk that road of fear and uncertainty, this Easter morn gives us hope and joy in the same way it gave these to Mary Magdalene. We can walk without fear. We have a Savior who is truly risen..."

He continued speaking his words of inspiration and Luke went from applying the words to Cliff to taking them upon himself. Was it this risen Christ who had walked the long and fearful road with him? Wasn't it Cliff who rescued him from Porterfield, Jennifer who snatched him from the jaws of despair…?

"We need to understand where God is to be found," Nugent went on. "Where his voice is heard, his help is offered, and his gifts given; whose hands, eyes, ears and touch he utilizes… look around you…"

Luke's comprehension resembled an incandescent light bulb. After hours and hours of helping Cliff study, he knew what Cliff now believed. And in exchange for that belief, Cliff was to receive some extraordinary gifts. Namely, the Holy Ghost with an array of virtues Luke thought Cliff already possessed, like wisdom and fortitude, knowledge and understanding, until Cliff had explained to him that all these gifts are spiritual. Still, Luke thought him already in possession of them, but who was he to argue with God.

Miss O'Brien, looking dignified and serene in a prim navy blue dress and matching hat, took her place as Cliff's sponsor as she stood behind him with her small hand placed upon his broad shoulder. As she returned to her seat, Ruth O'Brien was radiant.

Then the most extraordinary thing of all. Cliff was to receive his first Holy Communion, the body of Christ, although it looked like a flat disc of dried bread. Luke appreciated a good mystery, but this one was truly hard to grasp. It was beyond comprehension. His, at any rate. Cliff once reminded him that faith – faith in anything (including that flat white disc it seemed) – is about believing what you cannot necessarily see or understand.

"It makes you strong, Luke. Faith *has* made you strong…"

He accepted that, because it was true. He possessed more faith than he realized. He was encouraged by Cliff recognizing it. Things got hard sometimes, holding on when you didn't understand, when you couldn't see, when doubt took hold. Such as when Jennifer left.

Bathed in light from the sunlit stained glass, on his long desired Easter day, lifted up after his disappointment and hurt over Emmaline, Cliff got a holy glow about him. It suited him. And it seemed reasonable to think Cliff wanted to be as close and thankful to the One in whom he'd found comfort and relief in his trials as Luke wanted to be close to Jennifer whom he loved and missed beyond measure.

At the end, Cliff came away with a fancy-looking certificate documenting that he had acquired yet another name to his already lengthy handle – *Patrick* (his Confirmation name, after good old St Patrick, the man with the breastplate, no less).

Afterwards he opened his house for a huge party, quenching long thirsts.

Everyone came. Almost a whole churchful of folks. They ate and drank for hours, mostly drank, and Ethan was heard to say, "These Catholics ain't shy of a bottle or two, are they?" Whereupon Sara was heard to reply, "So, you've thinking of converting, Ethan?"

Cliff presented Ruth Barlow with a gift of appreciation. A small golden crucifix on a gold chain. It made her cry; she couldn't accept it. But he told her it was to stay around her neck and she wasn't to sell it. She promised, and Cliff had a way of making people keep their promises. And a strange thing… on the Saturday, after the reception at the Mayor's, Cliff received a small box by registered mail. There was no note, only the words *to be opened on Easter* scribbled on the inside wrapping.

"When are you going to open yesterday's mystery parcel?" Luke asked as he helped with the last of the straightening up after the party. "Who's it from, anyway?"

"Haven't a clue. May as well open it now." Cliff fetched it from his room. The wrapping contained a velvet box and inside sat a shining, solid gold crucifix and chain. Larger and heavier than Ruth's. A man's crucifix. Stunned, they both stared at it for a full minute before Cliff lifted it from the box. The polished gold of the cross caught the light from every direction as the poignant figure of Christ, arms stretched wide, caused them both to swallow hard.

"Who would send you that?"

"I've no idea."

"Emmaline?"

"Ah, no. Roberts doesn't believe in staying in contact."

"Who else knows then?"

"You?"

"No, my gold ain't even out of the ground yet. Besides, if I'd thought of it, I would've just given it to you, not send it."

It remained a mystery. Cliff wasn't all that good with unsolved mysteries; he had to know. Maybe someday…

The future was now spreading itself out like the never-ending grasslands around Laramie in summer, a restless green-gold ocean, swaying as far as the eye could see into the familiar territory of *vague maybes* and sweeping onwards over the horizon to the unknown lands of *no idea and anything could happen*. No longer something to be imagined, and once unthinkable, the future was startling – and unavoidable.

Charlie Quaid published a story in Monday's Tribune about Cliff's citation and his resignation. Cliff received hundreds of messages and letters of congratulations; so many, in fact, he paid the newspapers to publish a letter of gratitude to everyone for their kindness, their support, and for the honor of being their sheriff.

The first installment of Emmaline's *Empire for Liberty* ran in Wednesday's edition of the Tribune. It was an immediate success. Quaid was swamped by people's interest and promised his readers there was more to come.

"Funny how it seems like such a long time ago now," Luke was drawn to remark.

"Didn't think Roberts knew us that well, did you?" Cliff said dryly. It hadn't escaped Luke's notice that *Roberts* had replaced *Emma* whenever Cliff spoke about Emmaline.

"I wonder if Quaid is in contact with Emmaline."

"He'd be crazy not to. She's going to make him a lot of money."

Luke thought a good deal about Emmaline that day; what she was doing, was she happy, was she healthy again? He'd like to know, but did that make him disloyal to Cliff? Loyalty was a minefield in these cases; so he shelved his curiosity for the time being and kept his focus. It was hard – *Empire for Liberty* stirred him up inside; it was moving to see their experiences and struggles in words, a story for all to read. Meanwhile, Cliff gave nothing away, but he had to be feeling something.

Caroline and Richard returned to Omaha in the week following Cliff's conversion. They took Ben and Raina with them. Ben said he would return once he'd helped Raina find her mother.

"Don't dig up the quartz ore without me," he yelled from the window of the train.

The train withdrew from sight, leaving a hole in the horizon.

The day after that, John, Amy, Tressa and Adam took the train to Laramie, heading home. He wasn't sure when he would see them next and the notion made him uncertain yet again about this future they were all experiencing.

At the depot, Tressa had hugged him hard, saying, "You know what you have to do. Don't worry about us, please, just do it."

But he worried about her future, too.

A lot.

And Adam's.

Mac heard from Chase Deloight that Lamont had been released from the territorial prison in Laramie and had gone to find Eva Tarrant and Dillon Kerr. Cliff said news of that meeting would be worth waiting for.

But Cliff didn't wait. He began to pack up his house and prepare the town for his departure. Mac was made Sheriff until the elections. It was more than likely Mac would win that position in his own right.

One night Cliff called around at Luke's, a bottle of whiskey in hand. He opened that fresh bottle of Old Crow and poured two drinks.

"So," he said, "when are you going after your wife?"

Luke had to slurp before he could answer. "I don't know what happened with her father. I don't know what she wants."

"Are you nuts or something?"

"That's not funny, and I don't know why she won't write me."

"Go and find out."

What was she trying to tell him by keeping him in the dark?

Two days after the Keatons left town, Ethan came to him and said it was time that he took Sara, Tip and the Severinis home; he and Sara had made the arrangements.

"You and Sara?"

Ethan frowned hard. "You remember your mama, the woman who raised you, goes by the name of Sara…"

Luke rolled his eyes. "So you're leaving town…"

"Yep. Gonna have a poke around for that quartz ore." Ethan couldn't wait to get back and who could blame him.

"Sure, Ethan."

"Seems strange thinking that you live here now as well."

And it did seem strange, except that living in Cheyenne meant he should be with Jennifer. He was gonna be left here.

When he saw them off at the depot, Sara begged him outright to go to Provincetown, no matter what the outcome with Dermot.

"If the Faradays aren't worried about hearing nothing from Jennifer, why should you be? They have faith in her, where is yours? Luke, you are newlyweds. She wants to know you love her."

"She knows."

"You're being stubborn. You can't have everything your own way. Plain as day, she wants to tell you herself, not in a letter. This goes much deeper than a letter. How can you not see that?"

Indeed. What was the matter with him?

Ethan gave him a dig in the ribs. "Some advice she got right for once."

Even so, Sara quietly argued with Ethan about something until they got on the train. They never used to argue so much.

But Ethan got off again. He put his arms around him; hugged him hard. "Go and be happy, Luke. That's all you gotta do."

Luke's eyes stung with tears and he couldn't speak.

Ethan grinned and gripped the side of his face. "Just be happy. That's your job now. *That's* your job. And then everything will be all right. Trust me on this." And he left him.

"Ethan…" but the train was steaming up… "Ethan."

A beloved head appeared from a window. "What?"

"I'll be seein' ya."

Ethan grinned and threw up his hand. "Be seein' ya, son."

On what was supposed to be one of Cliff's last nights in town, Cam and Meg held a private farewell dinner.

While Meg commandeered Cam's help in the kitchen, before Mac and Pat arrived, he and Cliff sat talking for a spell in the parlor.

"So, Luke, let's make a deal. I'll take the Burlington east to Chicago where I'm headed and you take the UP south and then East where you're bound to be headed – *tomorrow*. We'll leave town same day. It's high time we were both moving on. And I'm not leaving you here by yourself."

"*Tomorrow!* Me?"

"Yep. You. Leave town. Find Jennifer. Starting tomorrow."

"I'll think about it."

"Don't take too long. You're going tomorrow."

"I said I'll think about it."

Cliff reached inside his coat pocket and pulled out a train ticket. "My way of saying thanks. I have you to thank for being where I am, and I want you to be where you should be. So, my parting gift to you. Kansas City via Denver. After that you're on your own."

"I don't know what the hell you are talking about, I don't need a gift from you, and I haven't packed up the house."

Meg walked in as cool as you please, like she'd heard every word from the kitchen, or knew about the plan. "Oh, we'll do that for you, Luke. Constance and I. In any case, you won't be gone all that long. Won't be any trouble. A few dust covers and we're done!"

He took the ticket.

The following morning Cliff came by.

"Ready?"

"As I'll ever be." But his insides were flapping and quivering like the wings of a hundred butterflies and a thousand dragonflies.

"Where's your luggage?"

"Right here."

Cliff frowned. "Saddlebags. Is that the best you can do?"

"What's wrong with my saddlebags? They go where I go. Hold everything I need. Where's your luggage?"

"Already on board. Took it down earlier. I have…more than you. Tell me then how you fit everything into your saddlebags?"

"Sure," Luke grinned, "on the way…"

They headed off to the depot together even though his train was scheduled to leave before Cliff's.

Cam was waiting for them. "This is it then."

They looked at each other, forced to feel the moment and saved from having to suffer more of it by the conductor on Luke's train calling to his passengers.

"Be seeing you, Cam." He and Cam shook hands.

"Give my love to George. See you when you come home." As usual, the words were not uttered without clear intent. "You have the address I gave you?"

"Yeah. Thanks."

"Godspeed, Luke." But Cam saw through him at that point. "You have something you want to ask me, so ask it."

"Will you keep an eye on the Keatons while I'm gone? When all's said and done, they got a lot more grieving that needs doing."

Cam raised a reassuring hand. "I know you're worried about them, but Meg and I will not neglect them, I promise." His hand rested on Luke's shoulder, firm with encouragement. "Now go be with George and bring her home."

It seemed so simple when Cam said it like that. And it sounded a lot like *go and be happy, that's your job now.*

Maybe when he got on the train he could genuinely entertain the concept. Maybe he could finally be free of the shadows and walk in the light. Maybe hope was on that train.

Cliff, meanwhile, was eyeing his ride on another line. "Weird, eh? Leaving, after watching everyone else leave."

Attuned to an uneasy sense of how huge the gap in his life was going to be without Cliff, Luke half-grinned. He owed Cliff more than he could ever repay; he wouldn't be alive without him. They shook hands. There was too much to say, and even then it was too hard to say it. So they mumbled... *Stay in touch. Have a safe journey.*

Cliff was about to do something remarkable in his life that very few people knew about and that deserved a sincere and hearty, "Good luck."

"Thanks. I would say the same to you but you won't need it."

Cliff was a man of faith; he was urging Luke to be one, too, no matter what.

With a final nod, Luke tore himself away and stepped straight on the train without looking back. He stowed his saddlebags on the rack above his seat and was grateful to be sitting on the far side of the train…

After what seems like a long while, the train pulls out of Cheyenne. He is leaving at last. And there is nothing to go back to, not without Jennifer and Evan.

He wipes his face on his sleeve as Cheyenne finally slides from his grasp.

Cliff

"You'd better get aboard," Cam urges him. "The engine is not the only thing steamed up…"

Cliff gives a smile as his conductor, Rhys Fuller, aka 'Grouchy Baller' (he used to play baseball until he wrecked his knee and the old Doc told him his ball-playing days were over), strides up and down the platform, with an ever so slight limp, frowning.

"Mac said he'll be here, Cam – he will be."

Sure enough, one time deputy and now Sheriff McNamara comes towards them. He thrusts out his hand at once. Cliff takes it, gripping hard and fast.

"Guess the day had to come," Mac says.

"I'm going to miss you, Mac."

"In a city like Chicago?"

"Wherever I am, you know that."

"Reckon I'll spare a thought for you every so often. Now, don't worry about the place, I'll take care of her. Make you proud."

"I'm already proud. Couldn't have asked for a better partner. Thank you, Mac."

"Aw, get on the train. You forgetting you thanked me already? – hundred times at least. And eat once in a while, for God's sake."

Chuckling, Cliff says, "I'll be back to check up on you."

"I'm thinking we'll still be here – right, Cam?"

Cam slides his hands into his pockets. "It's very likely."

Mac gives a firm nod. "Now get on that train…"

Cliff gives it a sidelong glance. For five years he always got on a train with the knowledge he would be coming back.

"It ain't forever," Mac says. "You'll come visit."

"Been a long time since I was there."

"Five minutes and it won't feel so strange."

"You think?"

"Journeys often end up where they began," Cam says.

"Now there's a piece of philosophy," Mac grins.

"Guess I have been on a journey…"

Cam chuckles. "Never a truer word."

He nods, with a hollow sigh, feeling the strangeness of no man's land.

"All aboard!" Grouchy steps up to him. "Including you, Mr Ryan, you ain't sheriff no more, and we got no call to hold up the train for the general public…" He strides off, leaving Mac and Cam to wipe grins off their faces and him to ponder how quickly five years of service and a citation can amount to nothing for some.

"All the times I can recall you jumping on or off a moving train just trying to get the job done," Mac mutters.

Cam chuckles. "There'll be no more of that. Good bye, Cliff…"

They shake hands, the tight grasp of Cam's telling him how much he'll be missed.

"It didn't end so badly, did it?" Cliff remarks.

Cam pulls a wry grin. "The Territory remained on its feet."

"And not a circuit court in sight."

"Nor one horse towns."

He looks from one to the other one last time. Living, working, and almost dying in Cheyenne had shaped his destiny; now that destiny hovers on the horizon as though it has been waiting for him. The time had come to fulfil it.

"I'll be in touch," he promises.

"Sure you will," Mac says. "Safe journey. Make us proud, Cliff."

He aims to; and he will.

And he does what he watched Luke do, understanding the necessity of it; he tears himself away and boards the train without looking back.

Emmaline

Orlando, Florida
The Roberts' household
It being a sparklin' spring day an' all...

The morning mail arrives. She greets their letter carrier, the erudite Teddy Wannamaker, on the porch where he hands her a bunch of letters while wearing a grin reflecting the sunny nature of the day.

"You look fine today, Miss Emmaline. And there's a good-looking envelope from Cheyenne in Wyoming Territory for you."

She locates it in the bunch, recognizing the handwriting at once. "Thank you, Teddy. I look forward to opening it right this minute. And thanks for being so patient with me all these weeks. "

"It's my job to help put anxious folks at ease. Best kinda day is when I can do that. I sure have an auspicious feeling about that one. Take good care of yourself now." Teddy tips his hat and moves on.

She hurries inside.

With a tight grip on the plumpish packet addressed to her in Mr Quaid's handwriting, feeling more excited about it than she has felt about anything for quite some time, she tosses the other letters on the hall table and scoots off to her room. The contents include neatly folded pages from the Tribune, a letter and a healthy check.

Mr Quaid writes:

Dear Roberts,

Hope this finds you well again. You gave me quite the scare. I hope the balmy Florida climate has seen you to rights again because I hate to think of one of my best reporters in anything less than tip top condition and always ready to pounce on the next great story. And as you can see with your very own eyes, I bought new typewriting machines, for all of us. Thought you'd appreciate it more than my handwriting. Who wouldn't, right?

All goes well here. You wouldn't know the place. The ice and snow have melted. It's actually warm for part of the day – about one o'clock for fifteen minutes. Young Zac wanted me to tell you he's sorry you're not here to experience it.

You'll find enclosed that bonus check I promised you upon the publication of part one of Empire for Liberty. The reaction was beyond my expectations. People want more. There's a kind of fever here now for anything to do with the Alliance and the Bodecker trial. It helps that Faraday won all his cases, but you of all people knew he would. Still, sorry you couldn't be here for the dramatic conclusion. I have included the first edition of Empire for Liberty. Thought you might like it. I'll send the rest as we publish.

It's starting to get quiet in town these days and easy to believe the whole drama never took place. I don't know if you want that summer job this June, but it's waiting for you. The town would be more than happy to see you back, especially now that nearly all the players in our little drama are gone.

However, there's one other thing. So listen up, Roberts, something I can tell now you about Ryan, who he really is. I don't think you know, because if you did you wouldn't have left the way you did...

❖

Time to face facts. He isn't coming; he never had any intention of doing so. Resolutely, she vows that the foolish tears rolling down her cheeks will be the last she ever sheds over the matter; tears that had filled up the empty space where he was – and no longer is.

Dear Jennifer,

    How are you and Luke? I miss you both a great deal.

    I've been doing everything precisely as you prescribed and feeling so much better. Dr Anson here is very impressed with you, and with Amy, too. I am very curious now as to your progress into discovering how to winter-proof me! Do you have any news to report? It's probably much too soon, I know, but as you can see I am very keen to get my life back on track, and pursue the opportunities that come my way regardless of the climate in which they present themselves. Excuse my enthusiasm, I do not wish to rush you.

    Now I must broach a difficult subject. Regarding Cliff, I understand that you may feel inclined to write about him, but I must beg your favor here and insist that we never mention him in our letters, not in passing or for any reason at all. While there is much to treasure from my time in Wyoming, some things need to be put aside forever so life can go on. I <u>cannot</u> hear about him if I am to succeed. I feel sure you understand and I thank you from the bottom of my heart for being my friend.

    Of course, I long to hear <u>your</u> news. Everything here feels very different to me now, so tame and orderly after my experiences in Wyoming, so any news from your neck of the comparatively wild woods would be most welcome! I believe Wyoming gets into your blood.

    I do so hope you are well, my friend. Give my best regards to Luke.

Affectionately,

Emmaline

Cliff

"You sure you want this job?"

"I'm sure."

"You're a lawyer, you say?"

"Among other things, yes."

"Hear Chicago is one tough town. Is that why you left?"

"No, it's not. And I hear Cheyenne is a tougher town."

"She's tough. Better than her early days, but she's got a ways to go before she's tamed. You think you're the man?"

"Takes more than one man, don't you think, to tame a whole town."

"Reckon maybe it does. You look young. How old are you?"

"Old enough."

"Sharp as a whip, ain't ya. Okay then. You can start Monday morning. The pay ain't much."

"It'll be enough. Sheriff, I noticed a house for sale on 19th and Ransom. Who do I see about buying it?"

Strange how some of his first moments in Cheyenne play over in his head as the train speeds into his hometown – part of the process of getting things straight in his own mind he supposes, letting go, making room...

The train passes through neighborhoods that weren't there five years ago, as well as giving him eye-opening views of diverse industry that has sprung up since he once lived here. As it moves closer to central Chicago, the train stops at stations packed with workers, families, businessmen, indeed, citizens of all persuasions.

Billboards on station walls advertise everything from popular stores to the latest sure-fire remedy to the next rally planned by the industrial workers for an eight-hour workday.

He disembarks at Grand Passenger Station, which wasn't here when he left five years ago. Grand though it may be, already it looks like a child who's outgrown his new clothes. Situated on Canal Street, on the east bank of the south branch of the Chicago River, with the red brick elegance of three pavilions stretched between Madison and Adams, and basically in the center of town, the station is teaming with every kind of humanity.

After a five-year absence, humbled by Chicago's size and vigor, for a moment he forgets he's not a native of frontier Cheyenne. It dawns as a peculiar revelation that *this* is his town, this tough, gritty and yet somewhat gilded metropolis on which he turned his back five years ago. He needs to get that sorted quickly; sure Cheyenne was a life-altering chapter in his life, and will always hold a special place in his heart, but in all that time, through all his adventures and trials, successes and losses, he has never stopped being a Chicagoan. And that, at this point, is crucial.

Out in the street, and onto the wide concourse from the station, the hub of city life explodes into being. People, hundreds of them. Trolleys, trams, rigs, hacks and carriages. Everything is on the move. There is no looking off into the distance and contemplating mountains or plains or ancient horizon. He can't even see the Chicago River, although he can sense it, mostly through his nose, and he'll have to cross it soon enough. For now, its south branch forms the busy canal behind the station. As for his nose, the smells of industry in its relentless pursuit and of humanity at its most intense are making themselves at home.

Meanwhile, the heat of all that striving negates any lingering spring chill off Lake Michigan. Anyway, he hasn't forgotten that by the beginning of May the city has seen off the winter and summer is on the way. After the winter he's been through, this is indeed a welcome prospect.

His blood begins to flow fast in his veins as his heart responds to the rousing pulse of the city.

The old newspaper-stand is still conveniently located adjacent to where the cabs line up. He picks up a copy of The Globe, hands over the money and tucks the paper under his arm before he steps into a cab.

"Ryan House," he tells the driver. "Prairie Avenue..."

"South Side," the driver says amiably. "Prairie Avenue it is. We'll head on over and take a drive down Michigan Avenue and be there in no time. Always a pleasure to venture into that part of town."

Although he spoke as though he had all the time in the world, the driver demonstrates skill and pace in the whirling activity of downtown Chicago.

Cliff rethinks his intention to read the paper on the way as he quickly realizes he needs to reacquaint himself with his city. Where he expected to see a particular thing, something else had replaced it; one-time vacant lots are filled to capacity; single or double story buildings are now towers in comparison; city blocks he was once completely familiar with he is struggling now to recognize. Buildings, bridges, businesses. Construction is prolific. Chicagoans are nothing if not good at construction (after the Great Fire and the Chicago that rose from those ashes who'd dare dispute it). And yet why should he be surprised – the city is always changing, becoming more, pushing the boundaries. That was true when he lived here, but he's missed out on five years and it's eye-opening even for him.

This is a true city, where people work and live and strive and enterprise (with varying shades of legitimacy and equity) on a scale unmatched. Heritage and progress side by side. And everyone at loggerheads as to whether people come before commerce. You can select the truth from which ever shade of gray you prefer; there's a lot to choose from. Only one other city in America is greater; New York City. Since New York is older than Chicago by two hundred years, who could care less? The Windy City is one of the fastest growing cities in the world (that hasn't changed), with a character unique to her. And every structure expresses her outrageous self-confidence. Behold Chicago! Behold a city without equal.

Then, with the calm and stately appearance of the residential mansions along Michigan Avenue, with 'home' not far away now, familiarity creeps up on him, gradually reclaiming the years of absence and in turn creating a conflicting response; his emotions pull hard towards Cheyenne, reaching for the recent familiar. But there is no going back... no matter how strong his desire to return to those moments with her in Quaid's office, obliterate the option he gave her to choose and instead tell her outright what she needed to know about him, and say to her *I'm going home, I belong in Chicago, and I believe with all my heart that you belong there with me,* all that is in the past. Going back is not an option. He is here to stay. And he *will* stay. And with every passing moment, all that is familiar or new to his eyes becomes his reality, his present and his future, his tomorrows and forevers, because *this* city will define him. Of that he is certain.

With the newspaper rolled up in his coat pocket, he deposits himself on Prairie Avenue's sidewalk, looking up at the house.

Yep. The house is exactly the same. As for the rest of Prairie Avenue, its residents appear to have done very well for themselves.

"She's a fine street, no denying," the driver remarks. "Chicago's finest some say."

And as far from the frontier as you could possibly imagine.

"You live in there?" the driver continues, taking Cliff's luggage from the hack and placing it by his feet. "That's the Ryan House. You a Ryan?"

"You've heard of the Ryan family?"

"The Ryan family who lives in *that* house? Who hasn't?"

Silly question.

"Just so happens my brother's worked over at The Globe for years. Takes care of the presses. But everyone knows the current Ryan – Phillip – is only temporarily looking after things, till the real heir returns."

"What's your brother's name?"

"Who wants to know?"

"Fair enough," Cliff concedes. "You were saying..."

"The heir to The Globe is supposed to return, take up his position left to him when his father died, that'd be about twelve years ago. Phillip Ryan is a cousin, second in line."

"And the father?"

"You pulling my leg? Only a foreigner would'n've heard of

him – Dominick Ryan, the newspaper tycoon. Biggest man in town back in the day. Owned the three big papers in town. Founded one of his own – The Globe – and bought out the others. Supported one ideology and criticized the rest."

"What happened to him?"

"Politics, that's what. Inquest said it was an accident and the family and the board left it at that. But most folks believed different. Can't recall a single soul who didn't think it weren't a *politically motivated assassination* to get rid of him. That's the term that got bandied about. Ryan told too many people what to think and how to think. Terrible shame, his wife died, too. And the cousin's folks, Douglas and Charlotte Ryan. Left grandparents in charge of the boys. The papers had a field day with the whole affair. The inquest didn't go far enough, in my opinion. Ryan had serious enemies."

Cliff swallows hard; whatever cold, hard truth might be uttered about his father's death, and rumors abounded, his mother's passing will always be easy prey for his emotions. He clears his throat. "What happened to The Globe and the other newspapers?"

"When Ryan Senior died, there was a battle for control of the papers and his estate. The Board of the Ryan estate managed to hang onto The Globe. The Ryans lost the two other papers. But not the estate, or wealth, or all their other investments and holdings; not this house and not their reputation."

"Where did this heir get to?"

"When he finished college, he became a lawyer, and refused to take on his position on the Board. Never liked his father's politics. Who could blame him? But those cronies of his father wouldn't let him be and he wanted out. Rich folks got their own set of troubles. Anyway, rumor has it he went West. Somewhere on the frontier is what I heard. Indians, outlaws, cowboys. Get that."

"Sounds like some kind of legend the way you tell it."

"Guess it is in a way. The real heir is Ashcliff Ryan. You wouldn't be him by any chance?"

"An interesting question. Anyone living in the house now?"

"Mm, the cousin. The other Ryan house, Phillip Ryan's family home, down the street, burnt down a couple of months ago. The cousin got permission from the Board to live here till he rebuilds, so my brother tells me. Permission, get that! Family's family, but maybe it's different for rich folks. They got those trusts protecting everything down to the last silver teaspoon..."

Cliff feels the blood drain from his face. "Anyone hurt?

"In the fire? No. Some priceless works of art went up in smoke though. Douglas and Charlotte Ryan were collectors. Guess that's what rich folks do. Anyhow, if that's all..."

Relieved, Cliff pays him the cab fare and includes a substantial gratuity. "Thanks for the information."

"I reckon you are him, the heir. You seem familiar. Whether you are or you ain't, good luck to you. My brother's family been associated with The Globe for, oh, long time now. But I don't care for politics and so-called freedom of the press. I prefer to make up my own mind than be told what to think all the time. That's why I drive this rig." With that off his chest, he tips his hat and leaps up into his vehicle.

As he drives away, Cliff whips out The Globe from his pocket and unrolls it.

PERIL ON OUR STREETS! *ANARCHY!*
WORKERS MAKE OUTRAGEOUS DEMANDS.
FOREIGNERS ARE TAKING OUR JOBS!
SOCIAL REFORMERS ASSAULT CITY HALL.
WORK OR BE SACKED, WARN BOSSES.

The cab driver is correct; nothing has changed at The Globe.

The house cannot be viewed in one glance; it takes time and a diligent scan with a keen eye to take it all in, and even then that's only the front. It's not that he doesn't appreciate the house and its uniqueness; so it's over-sized and sometimes on the dark side, but as mansions go, it's okay. His mother's good taste mostly holds the upper hand in all its aspects, and he would stridently argue with anyone who said otherwise. She lingered for a month in her room before she passed away and he kept it the way it was until the day he left Chicago; he assumed it has remained her room since. Those last weeks and days with her he can vividly recall, since he spent them at her bedside; he begged her to recover, for his sake if not her own. But every day hope faded; and when the end came he vowed he would never let anyone he knew succumb to despair. *Hopefully,* she didn't follow his father to the place where over-opinionated, ambitious, politically reckless and brilliant men go when they die, although she would always follow wherever Dominick Ryan trod; is that kind of loyalty rewarded even if it was misplaced at times? Any man should be so blessed to marry such a woman; despite his many faults, his father must have considered himself so.

Having mounted the great stone and marble stoop, he has arrived on the front porch. The impressive double entrance doors loom before him. Oh, how strange this all feels. Too many feelings... best to take each moment as it comes.

Without him making any signal of his arrival, one door opens. A quaint and decrepit fellow appears from behind it, complete with suit pressed shiny after countless years of service. And the old eyes light up and the wrinkled face comes to life.

"Master Ashcliff?"

He grins at the old man, the warmth of affection and reunion filling him up. "Hello, Coop, how are you?" He steps forward and takes the old man's bony hand, clasping it between both of his. Coop places his other hand on top and a river of reconnection flows through him. He's home.

"As I live and breathe..."

"How long have you been doing that now, Coop?"

Coop chuckles. "Could be seventy-two years, could be more."

More like eighty-two. "Ever heard of retirement?"

Coop pulls the door wide by taking tiny backward steps. "I told your father back then I'd leave the Ryan employ when I died and I meant it."

"Same old Coop."

"*Tsk.* Same old Ashcliff."

Cliff picks up his bags and enters the house.

Coop is chuckling behind him as he closes the door. "Hasn't changed, has it?"

It even smells the same.

"It's like going back in time. Except she's not here."

Coop grunts in a good-natured way. "Everyone needs a place to go back to and draw from. Even you."

Cliff dumps his bags, removes his hat, smiling at the old fellow.

Coop shakes his head. "Look at you. You're a man now," he grins, waging a finger in Cliff's face. "Your grandmother, God rest her soul, wouldn't recognize you."

Unbuttoning his coat, Cliff says, "Whatever you say, old man."

Coop takes his coat and walks off with it, mumbling, "Stay there for a bit so I can tell the mistress you're here."

"Which mistress would that be?"

"Master Phillip's wife."

"Flip *married?*"

Coop waves a dismissive gesture and keeps walking, still mumbling; it sounds like, "Not cut out to be a bachelor that one..."

"Well, who did he...?"

He sighs and waits with a commendable degree of curious patience, after all this is his home and he wants to tear through every room and reacquaint himself with everything in it. Very soon, though, a pretty dark-haired young woman with a stony expression glides into the entrance hall. Coop is behind her; no gliding there.

"Here he is, Mrs Ryan," Coop announces, with some kind of oddly grand hand gesture. "In all his returning splendor..."

"You are Phillip's cousin?" she asks.

"Yes, Ma'am. Cliff."

Her eyes go wide. "*You* are Ashcliff Ryan?"

He steps forward. "How do you do? I'm sorry we've not met before. Always hoped Flip would find ..."

"Phillip isn't here."

"I didn't catch your name, Ma'am."

She stiffens. "I didn't give it."

Coop grunts. "It's Mrs Ryan."

Cliff bites his tongue.

"His old room, Mrs Ryan?" Coop asks as he bends over one of Cliff's bags.

"Don't touch those!"

"Eh?"

"This gentleman isn't staying, Cooper."

"Mrs Ryan, he *has* to stay. The house belongs to him. You can't kick Ashcliff Ryan, Dominic Ryan's heir, out of his own home."

Cliff settles his gaze on the woman before him. It's beginning to dawn on her she can't win. Her life, as she knew and preferred it, is about to change. And the prospect is making her tremble.

Coop gives a meaningful chuckle. "Better watch it or he'll tell *you* to leave."

Her chin tilts up even more; defiant little thing, she is. But in that moment he thinks he understands her.

Smiling, he says, "Coop, you're scaring my cousin-in-law."

"Beg pardon, Mrs Ryan," Coop says, "I'll send for Master Phillip, have him fetched here right away. Come on, Master Ashcliff. Let's find your old room. You had better take that larger case; never manage that one…"

Cliff gives a slight bow. "With your permission, Ma'am."

Her eyes flash; a terse nod follows.

Around half an hour later, with dust covers removed and some of his belongings unpacked, he is changing his shirt when his cousin charges into his room and stops dead in his tracks.

"My God, it's true…"

"You still haven't learned to knock, Flip."

"Cliff! I'm glad to see you."

"And you…"

They embrace heartily. Cliff's feels his chest fill up with emotion for the cousin who is more like his brother. He has never felt the difficulty of their five year separation more keenly than he does now, now that the span of time has come full circle.

"Heard about your house, Flip. Glad you weren't hurt."

"Thanks. Hope you don't mind putting us up like this…"

"As if I would. Stay as long as you want."

"Look at you!" Phillip exclaims suddenly. "A little beat up. What's that?"

Cliff starts buttoning his clean shirt over the tender scar of his recent wound. "Nothing for you to worry about. You look good, Flip. Really good."

"You've changed."

"You haven't."

With a laugh he steps back, giving Cliff room to finish dressing. "But I have, cuz! I have a wife."

"We met. Although she was reluctant to give me her name."

"She's… she is my Berenice. She was Berenice Hargreaves."

"The tea and coffee merchants Michigan Avenue Hargreaves?"

"Your sabbatical hasn't affected your memory."

"She's as pretty as her name, but she looked horrified to see me. What have you been telling her about me?"

"That you're a wild man who would one day come home to take back what is rightfully his."

Cliff meets his cousin's glance across the room. "Children?"

"We've only been married six months."

"And it suits you. I offer my warmest congratulations." He chuckles at Flip's softening expression.

"I'll accept them, if you mean it."

"Why wouldn't I? It certainly isn't easy to find the woman of your dreams these days."

"No."

And keep her…

"So, what brings you back?"

"Business."

Phillip stiffens, but not like his wife. There's a certain manner members of the Ryan clan adopt when it comes to business.

"Will you relax?"

And Phillip does, up to a point. "So what business?"

Cliff threads his arms into his waistcoat and starts buttoning. "I know exactly what I want. What I *don't* want is to run the board."

"You have a position there you had to take up once you came home, that was the agreement we made."

"Anyone discontented with the way you run things?"

Phillip frowns, confused. "No, but…"

"Good. Let's keep it that way."

Phillip's frown becomes almost endearingly quizzical. "Then what do you want?"

"I want the board to make me Managing Editor of The Globe."

The frown darkens to utter bewilderment. "You hate the paper. You've hated it since I can remember."

"I hated what my father did with it. But lately I've had a chance to think about what *I* want to do with it."

"We have a perfectly good managing editor now."

Cliff picks up The Globe from his bed. "This is the same outrage The Globe has been churning out since my father founded it. I want it to change."

Phillip goes understandably quiet for a moment. Then, "I thought you became a *lawyer* in order to change the world. What do you know about running The Globe?"

Cliff's turn to frown. "That's an odd thing to say."

"All right, yes, it is… I guess what I really meant to say is that you've been gone a long time."

"Nothing a little catching up can't fix."

"What have you been doing all this time? By the look of you, not running a newspaper."

"Not… exactly."

Before he left Chicago, he and Phillip made an agreement; the break would be without ties. He needed to find out who he was and where he belonged; no communication with home. Only then would he know that if he experienced the compulsion to return, it was right.

"Flip, I want The Globe."

"Why?"

"I have my reasons and I promise I will share them with you. So, we find the current man another job, or sack him."

"I'll have to run it by the board."

"We already have two votes. Yours and mine."

Phillip sighs, dragging his hand down the back of his head. "Back five minutes and you're already giving orders. What happened to you? You look like you've lived a whole other life…"

He straightens the collar of his coat. "I guess I did. I'll tell you about it soon, I swear. For now, let's get down to business."

"No," Phillip says firmly, "let's get you settled in first. You look tired and that injury on your side looks recent."

He also relents. "All right. We'll start fresh in the morning."

Phillip nods. Relaxes. And smiles. "I *am* glad to see you, Cliff. I thought you were never coming back."

Cliff returns the smile. "You just never know what's on the horizon."

Luke

The train moves through the city, steadily chewing up the outskirts. So, this is St Louis, the original gateway to the West. She's an old city, famous and large, much older and grander than Cheyenne. An icon of a bygone era, with her French roots. Everybody knows that until the railroad came along her lifeblood was the biggest river in America. The Mississippi. Maybe he ought to make an effort to find his way down to the levee and take a gander at it and the riverboats, but sightseeing is not uppermost in his mind. He'll have to cross the river anyway, if Jennifer is still on the other side.

In times gone by, wagon trains of liberty-loving Americans and immigrants congregated here before they began their westward trek to settle the Great Plains and beyond, much to the dismay of people already living there, namely the tribes, many of whom had previously been forced into the west by European settlement of the east... So, sure, he is able to see both sides, he's in a unique position. Considering the cost, he doesn't want to dwell.

He's gotta *try* not to think so much. How many times has Ethan told him that in his life? *If I had a penny for every thought you had, I could own half the country. Just go with life, son, you can't change everything, only what you can, and one thing you can't change is the past. One eye on the past, but both eyes on the present.*

What about my mind's eye?

Smart ass. You'll keep.

He grins to himself.

There's a rush of people when he steps off the train. As he maneuvers through the crowd, he secures his saddlebags over his shoulder and fixes his hat.

He receives a few curious glances... and...

"Look, Mama, a cowboy!"

"Hush, Amelia, he'll hear you."

The woman thinks he'd be insulted? Not proud?

He winks at the little girl as they pass each other and her giggles tickle his ears.

He hasn't worked the ranch in months, so what gave him away – the Stetson, boots and saddlebags? Fair enough. A cowboy he may be, but all his relatives and ancestors left their homes in the east and came through this town long ago, heading west. This place is a part of him, too. He's like the product of all that emigrating come to life. Maybe that's what Amelia saw; something authentic. Even Ethan'd have to like that thought.

Out in the busy street, he looks this way and that. Yep, another big city of fancy buildings, do-or-die commerce and hectic traffic; first was Denver, then Kansas City and now St Louis. If he could stop feeling so jittery about Jennifer, he might even be fascinated by the journey. Beyond is Illinois, Indiana, Ohio, Pennsylvania... all those states he learnt the names of in school and never thought he'd ever cross or visit. He has no idea which railroad to take next, but the person he's come to see will know... which railroad and he's hoping a whole lot more.

"You're new in town. Welcome, stranger." A black man dressed in a dark blue suit and matching peak-brimmed hat stands before him with his hand out for the saddlebags. It's impossible to tell his age. He flashes a smile. "My cab's right there, so where can I have the honor of takin' you?"

Yep, cities are all the same; always someone wanting to give you a ride in their cab. He intended to take a streetcar, but on second thought he wouldn't mind feeling the rhythm of that fine horse's gait and watching its black tail swishing as he rides behind in what looks like a simple vehicle, where it appears you can choose to sit inside or upfront with the driver.

He puts his hand on his saddlebags. "I'll keep these with me, if it's all the same to you."

A polite, deep chuckle. "O' course."

He fishes the address out of his pocket. "Petrie Avenue."

"That's outa town a ways, close to the University. Why don't you hop in, pilgrim, an' we'll be off."

He's never been one to ride in the back of anything on his own; when you've spent most of your life on the back of a horse, you get used to the view and the fresh air on your face.

"Like to ride up there with you, if that's okay."

"Be my guest."

Along cobbled streets, they leave warehouses, brick'n stone buildings, the river, the levee and the bustle of downtown behind, and head into tree-lined streets with nice houses and neat gardens. The perfume of domestic life fills the air he breathes; it's comfortable and vibrant at the same time.

His driver's name is Ruben and he's a friendly character. He likes to talk, which is unfortunate since Luke's in the mood for thinking. When he's not with Jennifer, his head keeps right on thinking and won't let up, like he's searching for her; it all quietens, makes sense, when they are together; their hearts meet, and their minds meet; she is like the completion to all his thoughts.

As long as it's not about Dermot...

"So where d'you say you was from, Luke?"

"I didn't yet. Wyoming."

"That's kinda near Colorado, ain't it?"

"Kinda."

"I got folks in Colorado. They keep askin' me to come out to see 'em. They went there as free men after the war."

"Why don't you visit?"

Ruben gives his head a flick to the side. "Mebbe. But I jus' can't seem to go no more west than St Louis."

More west than St Louis... He couldn't imagine himself any more east than Cheyenne, but he'd been to Omaha; he'd got as far as Sedalia once when he and John were looking for Mart, but that almost doesn't count. Yet here he is. Going upstream, it feels like. He gets to thinking he'd have liked to have seen for himself St Louis in those times gone by, instead of having to picture Ethan's chaotic description of his one visit here a long time ago. It included a stark account of the buying and selling of slaves on the steps of the courthouse. Would he have liked to have witnessed that? He feels disgusted thinking about it. And then deeply sad. So many people perished in the war to end it. So much heartache and destruction. *One eye on the past, but both eyes on the present…*

"Hey, Luke, you still with me?"

He clears his throat. "Sure, Ruben."

"Thought I'd lost you. So, what d'you think of St Louis so far?"

"I bet you ask all your passengers that."

"Question's the same but people ain't. Get all kinda replies."

Ruben has a kind and noble face sitting beneath the peak of that hat of his, but it also has a pinched quality, and depth, and something else…

He realizes he's staring and stops. Half the time he can't help it; sketch-worthy faces fascinate him. "I reckon you gotta like talking to do this kind of work."

"Now that's a fact. I like it. I like it a lot. So, what d'you think of St Louis so far?"

Luke shrugs.

"A mystery man, huh?" Ruben suggests and chuckles.

"No. Gotta long road ahead of me, Ruben. I'm only stopping by in St Louis."

"Young fella like you… Chasin' a woman by some chance?"

"A good chance."

"Ah, good luck with that, friend."

"Would you drop me at the top of the street when we get there; I'd like to walk for a bit."

"I ain't got a problem with that. Ain't had a cowboy is this rig o' mine fo' a long time. And not one from Wyomin' as I recall…"

Can't seem to go no more west than St Louis.

"You were born here in St Louis, Ruben?"

"I reckon I was."

Mm. But he's not sure, not entirely. He was born a slave? So there are no records. "Your mama is here somewhere in St Louis?"

"I reckon she is. Reckon she might still be livin'."

"How old were you, if you don't mind me asking?"

"Five, or six mebbe..."

"I'm sorry, Ruben."

"Now why are you sorry?"

"Because it was wrong."

"I was good stock. So they took me away from her. I got sold. Worked in a rich man's house right here in St Louis, praise the Lord. Never had to work on the levee or on the boats. I never got sold down the river or I'd be dead. I gotta be thankful fo' that. Then, when I was a grown man, President Lincoln freed us and the war came. Terrible, terrible time. I shoulda left Missouri, but I jus' couldn't."

Ruben is older than he looks; for his mama to be alive after all she'd been through and after all this time, the chances are slim. But then, miracles do happen. And Ruben is clinging on for one.

"She's here somewhere, I tell myself, but it's a long time ago."

"I hope you find her someday."

"Been searchin' long time. Tell myself I'm jus' a stupid ol' black man and I give up fo' a time. Then it comes back to me, like a hauntin': she loved you, Ruben, and she cried like her heart was broke in half, tryin' to keep hold of you."

"You remember that?"

"Wish I didn't. But, you see, Luke, I can't leave St Louis. I can't leave her cryin' like that."

Luke looks at the houses passing by until he can trust himself to speak. "She'd be proud of you, Ruben, you're a free man making a good and honest living of your very own. You're proof that no one can own another human being because what's inside of you is yours and no one else's, only *you* can do what you do, it's a sacred thing, and for someone else to claim it, exploit it, or steal it from you, that's wrong."

Ruben gives a small chuckle. "You're sure some philosopher for a western man."

"I don't want you to be sad about your mama any longer, Ruben."

"I can tell you're feelin' my sadness fo' yourself. And I sure do appreciate that, but don't take that on, Luke. Lookin' at you, I'd say you got troubles enough of your own."

"Some."

"You think I should quit lookin' for her."

"I think you should find a place here in St Louis you know your mama would've liked to rest in peace for eternity, and put flowers there whenever you feel like it."

"You think she's gone."

"I think she's gone. She's not crying anymore, Ruben. She's at peace. She's looking down on you and she's happy and that's how she'll stay."

Ruben flicks a sideways glance at him. "Huh. Would you jus' listen to that white boy."

Luke grins at him.

Eventually, Ruben draws his cab to a halt.

"This here is Petrie Avenue, Luke. Pretty, ain't it? Jus' look at them trees. Ain't that a sight? You came at the right time."

Luke nods, staring down the avenue. It's pink.

"Famous fo' its plum blossom, Petrie is. Bet you didn't know that."

"Can't say I did. How much do I owe you, Ruben?"

"A dollar'll do."

Luke ponies up, giving him two dollars, then jumps down. "Keep the change. Include a few stems in that first bunch of flowers from me. And thanks, Ruben. That was a fine ride."

Ruben chuckles and hands him his saddlebags. "You're welcome, Western man. Thanks for the tip. They'll be roses now."

"Good." He reaches up to shake Ruben's hand. A strong, dark hand clutches his. "It was mighty fine meeting you, Ruben."

"And you. Good luck, Luke, with that woman o' yours."

Ruben, his tail-swishing horse and his cab move off and Luke stands on the sidewalk observing for a spell before he plucks up the courage to start walking into that pink cloud.

He decides that there is only one way to go about this. Plunge straight in. All this time he's been able to focus on Jennifer and leave the Sullivans out of it, but that was never going to be possible in the long term. He has to face them, or whoever's at home, not knowing what to expect.

As he follows the house numbers displayed by each front door, the avenue unfolds from one picturesque point to another. Perfect trees, perfect road, perfect houses. He imagines Tressa setting out her watercolors and sitting down to a perfect afternoon of painting, a thought that makes him smile and loosens the knot in his chest.

He stops at the gate of number twenty-four and peers at the house, picture perfect like its neighbors, big and tall with long windows and gabled ones on the attic floor. Lots of windows would mean lots of rooms, right? – so the perfect house for a family of seven. It looks loved and well-cared for. He seems to recall Jennifer mentioning the family had lived here about five years and Jeanne called it their 'forever home'.

The front garden looks like it couldn't wait for spring, full of shrubs, small sections of lawn, spring flowers, yellow and purple ones, and some pink, and some of those white Easter lilies Nugent had in the church for Cliff's initiation; it smells good, sweet and crisp, and there is a distinct buzz of bees at work.

As he releases the gate latch, a small and familiar head shoots up from behind a lavender bush on his right. He and the small head stare at one another. A bee whizzes past. A pair of blue eyes narrows on him.

"What do you want?" the head demands.

"You're a strange kinda guard dog."

"I ain't a dog. You know I'm a kid. What do you want?"

Luke folds his arms. "What's the matter with you, Finn Sullivan? No one wants to play with you, I bet."

"You take that back! I oughta be in school, but the doctor said something's the matter with me and I should stay home. It's a bunch of malarkey. AJ wouldn't keep me home for nothing and she's the best doctor there is."

"Are you contagious?"

"No. I'm just dangerous when I'm mad."

"I can see that. What's eating you?"

"What's it to you anyhow?" And without another word, Finn takes off into the house, yelling for his father.

Was he that strange when he was a kid?

He heads down the garden path and up the short front stoop to the porch where he waits patiently for someone other than Finn.

When Frank appears, he feels an odd mixture of relief and apprehension. Relief that if anyone knows the situation in Provincetown it's Frank, and apprehension at having to explain himself.

"Luke!" His brand new brother-in-law comes to meet him. And his hand is shaken warmly.

"Frank. Hope I'm not intruding."

"You can't be serious!"

"Er, I..."

"I am very, very glad to see you. And I apologize for Finn. He's out of sorts. Going through a trying phase regrettably. Something's bothering him but he can't seem to say what it is. Thought we'd give his teacher a break."

"He does seem mighty agitated about somethin'."

"Precisely."

Finn reappears on the front porch, declaring excitedly, "Wait till I tell Conor you're here!"

"Finn, your room, now."

"But Pa..."

But one look from Frank and the kid is slumping off, his head hanging down. Once he's gone, Frank's expression reverts.

"Please come on in, Luke. You've come a long way and it's great to have you here."

He moves slowly through the house on Frank's beckoning, surveying its comfort and its character, but even these are unable to see off his nervousness.

Frank is saying, "Jeanne is not at here at present; fetching Conor and Ariel home from school. Needed to speak with Finn's teacher. But she will be here soon. Davina is with her. And Caroline is napping in her room, although after Finn's performance I don't know how long that will last... Are you all right, Luke?"

He's surprised to find Frank studying him closely.

"Concerned about Jennifer. Haven't heard from her."

"Straight to the point."

He sighs. "Why not?"

"Indeed," Frank offers him a comfortable chair in the living room. "What can I get for you? A drink? I seem to recall last time we sat down together we had one."

Luke shakes his head and sits down. "Nothing, thanks."

"George hasn't contacted you at all?"

"Only a telegram to say you had arrived."

Frank's thoughtful expression has a slight smile attached to it. If he understands Jennifer's silence, then maybe he could share?

"I returned from Boston myself a week ago."

"And?"

"I had no idea you have been in the dark all this time. I assumed that George…"

"This is a test, ain't it?"

"After what she's been through, Luke, I can honestly say she wouldn't see it that way."

He swallows hard as he tries to fathom that. His head hurts at the prospect of having to unravel it.

Frank draws up a wooden chair opposite him; he sits down, and appears to be searching for the right words. "Dermot… my father died of tuberculosis the day after we got to Provincetown." He stops and looks at his hands. "He was waiting for her all that time."

The evil man is dead at last. Good riddance. Now Jennifer is free of him. He wants to give a whoop! But as he looks at Frank's unguarded face, looks at the brother who cared for Jennifer all her life, his conscience receives a prod. "I'm very sorry for your loss, Frank."

"Thank you. That is generous of you to say, considering. But I don't feel a loss, only that something which was exceedingly long and difficult and harsh has ended, and a sense of relief. Father was very ill. I don't know how he hung on, but he was determined to have her forgiveness before he died. He… he desperately wanted to be reunited with our mother and he believed he knew what he had to do."

This is too much! Damn that fucking man to hell. Luke springs to his feet. He walks to the other side of the room and back again.

182

Frank bursts out, "Would you say what is on your mind?"

"No." Luke rubs his forehead and repeats his walk. "I'm gonna swear… long and hard out loud…"

"Better you swear than wear a hole in my rug."

"Better the hole in your rug, believe me."

"I know how you feel about Dermot."

Luke stops pacing.

"I know it is something you can't help because of how you feel about George."

"How… how did she…?"

"She was incredible. And I have you to thank for it."

"Me? No, I think you must be mistaken." And he resumes his walk.

"Although I have been known to make the odd error from time to time, about this I am not mistaken. For someone who despised the man, you certainly gave her the most unexpected weapons."

"What do you mean by weapons?"

"She knew exactly how to break him down and get what she wanted. You see, Dermot wasn't expecting he would have to give her something in return. I could barely contain my glee. You taught her how to do that, don't deny it."

Luke stands still. What is he talking about? It quietly dawns on him. "Did Dermot love her as he waited for her to be born…"

Frank sits back, satisfied. "He admitted it. What a moment! Although he had a coup of his own at that point."

"A coup?"

"He guessed Jennifer is expecting a baby. I think he was very pleased about it."

"How… how did he guess about the kid?"

Frank smiles like an all-knowing math professor. "He said she would have to know how to approach such a deduction – she must be with child. All through her young life I taught her to survive my father by using her superior intelligence – logic, reason, deduction and plain old common sense. But only when she found you did she uncover the one weapon to truly disarm Dermot. Love, you see. But not hers for him – he destroyed any vestige of that years ago – but hers for you! What sublime irony!"

Luke needs to sit down. "No one else knows about the baby."

"George told me I could tell Jeanne and no one else until you both decide to announce it. Not even Joseph and Miles know. Luke, it is the very best news."

It's clear from Frank's expression that he is genuinely happy.

"Thanks."

"Luke, you gave George everything she needed for the job she had to do, you have to understand that."

"We were divided over her leaving."

"It doesn't matter anymore."

Luke inhales a deep breath and sighs it away. "And Dermot wanted her forgiveness, that's what all this was about?"

Frank nods. "And she granted it. She was strong, Luke. You made her stronger than she has ever been."

"I wasn't there!"

"They spoke of you, a great deal. Dermot formed a picture of you in his mind and I'd say it was quite an accurate one. And without you even being there, you stood up to him. Luke, what I am trying to say is that they formed a line of communication, an understanding if you like, through you. I asked her how she found the strength to forgive him. And she said it wasn't *her* strength; it was that you are her wellspring, in you she has more than enough joy and hope to share, even with Dermot."

Leaning forward, elbows on his knees, Luke jams his fists into his eyes. She loves him that much... so much that she was able to forgive Dermot... even forgive Dermot for his sake... "I have to go to her."

"And she is waiting for you. But tomorrow..."

"Now."

"Spend the rest of the day here and stay over one night with us. George would want that. And we want to get to know you better. George is safe. I wouldn't have left her otherwise. Joseph and Miles are only a few hours away. They promised to look in on her every other day. It's good for them to get to know one another better.

"There's something else you should know. George isn't staying at *Liberty Keep*. She rented a cottage in town, one she has always liked, and that's where she's staying. My father left her the house in his will, but she has refused it and I can't say I blame her. She has kept only two pieces from the house; our mother's portrait and a fruit bowl. None of us boys wants *Liberty Keep* either, so it will go up for sale. The money from the sale of the house will go to George. My brothers and I have insisted. One day she will know what to do with the money. A special bank account will be set up and it will be there when it's needed, with interest. Joseph is the executor of the will, so he is making all the arrangements.

"And finally, Dermot is laid to rest in the Provincetown cemetery with our mother. You wouldn't know she was buried there. None of us did till recently. Anyway, now they are together again. It's over. All of it. And I thank you, Luke, for your part in it because the conclusion was nothing I had ever imagined and so much more than I could have hoped for."

Luke takes his hands away and sits back. Everything's a blur for several moments, but this much is clear, "I really have to go to her."

Frank is calm but firm. "Tomorrow. You need to rest. And I'd like to know what happened in Cheyenne with the trial, how it ended. Luke, you are part of this family. We *are* interested in you, you know."

"I'm sorry. I don't mean to be..."

"You're not; it's a lot to take in."

Too true. His head's so full his mind is about to blank out. He steers his thoughts away from what awaits him in Provincetown to consider Frank's kind words and invitation.

That's a lotta family

You'll get used to it, besides you never know when you might need them

Their weddin' day. He'd never encountered a family like the Sullivans before. Or a brother quite like Jennifer's...

"Look, Frank, I'll be honest here..."

"Please, go ahead. I prefer things out in the open."

"Jennifer has you on a mountain that the rest of us mere mortals can't even begin to climb and..."

To his surprise, Frank starts laughing. "If I'm on a mountain, then you must be in the clouds." And his laughter deepens.

Luke watches him enjoy his own joke; not surprising Frank needed a good laugh in light of recent events.

A grin tugs at his mouth. Okay, so Frank's been thinking the same about him in return.

"The clouds, Frank?"

"Stratosphere, at least."

Luke scratches the back of his neck.

"Can we agree to meet on a lowly hilltop? Let George work out the rest?"

He grins. "I guess we can do that."

"So, you'll stay?"

"A home cooked meal and a bed that doesn't move would be welcome, thanks."

Still with a rogue chuckle, Franks says, "I'm glad we got that sorted out."

All at once there is an explosion of noise from the hall.

"Wow! Look at these! They're saddlebags! Who's here?"

"Conor," Frank sighs. "I have a feeling that boy belongs on a ranch. We may need to ask a favor of you in the not too distant future."

"Ask away," Luke chuckles.

In a flash, Conor appears at the living room entrance and then bolts into the room, barely stopping before he trips on the rug. "It *is* you! Wow! Wait till I tell Finn. Are you staying? Can you teach me about horses? AJ told me you draw them real well – can you teach me to draw 'em too?"

"Conor…" But that young face is so full of a child's innocent enthusiasm he has to swallow.

"Yes, sir?"

Sir? Mm… "First lesson. Horses like calm people."

"Oh… sure. I understand."

Ariel steps around her brother, dodging his long limbs like she's been doing it all her life. She comes straight towards him, lady-like and dignified, and reminding him of Jennifer.

"Uncle Luke," she says and he nearly falls off the chair.

"Ariel."

She smiles shyly. "You remembered my name."

"It's too intriguing to forget."

She giggles. "I hope you are well."

"I miss AJ," he confides.

"Me too. But you are here. Are you staying for supper?"

"If your mother will have me."

"Oh, she will. She likes you. Besides, you're family now, Papa said so."

Jeanne, with little Davina by her side, appears where Conor used to be. Her eyes are shining.

Luke stands. He feels Ariel's small hand slip into his and his heart skips a beat.

"Look who's here, Mama?"

Cliff

Seven days out of Cheyenne

Arnold Wexford tosses the last of his things into his carpetbag. "I want you to know that I resent this with every fiber of my being, Ryan."

"I'd feel the same in your shoes, Wexford, believe me. But you're not leaving empty handed, are you? And it's being written up in your favor."

"Really? The brat of Dominick Ryan returns to claim his inheritance and takes on the most senior position at The Globe. Well, sonny, editing The Globe wasn't supposed to be part of it."

"Says who? Oh, you mean the Board. But the Members of the Board saw it my way, didn't they?"

"Ever heard of professional courtesy, Ryan? – but then again, this game isn't your real profession, is it?"

"No, it's only my birthright."

Wexford gives a start, eyes him coldly and then snaps his bag shut. "Like father, like son."

Cliff says nothing more; he steps back and gives Wexford a clear exit path from the office of Managing Editor of The Globe. And when there is no longer a trace of Wexford to be seen or heard, he locates his assistant working at the desk outside his office, a man who reminds him of an older and somewhat dour version of Josh Bridger, spectacles and air of quiet efficiency included. Whether he possesses Josh's sense of optimism and ethical standards remains to be seen.

"Barnes, right?"

"Yes, Mr Ryan. Lewis Barnes."

"Pleased to meet you." They shake hands.

"And you." Barnes looks him straight in the eyes.

The dour clarity reveals a man of unapologetic purpose.

"You can tell me again when you've had a chance to really make up your mind."

"I won't need it, Mr Ryan."

"What's your story here at The Globe, Barnes?"

"I started as a lad in the basement with the presses when your late father rebuilt after the Fire. I've worked my way up to assistant to the managing editor, a post I've occupied for the past two years."

There can be no doubt that Lewis Barnes knows The Globe, and the people who work within her illustrious walls.

"Just the man I need then."

"What did you have in mind, Mr Ryan?"

Cliff bites back a grin. "Barnes, I want you organize a series of meetings across every department of the paper, starting with the editors. Editors in my office and everyone else wherever it's convenient for them."

"Timing, Mr Ryan?"

"Over the next forty-eight hours."

"Consider it done."

"Thanks. Oh, I will also need a full list and short profile of every reporter who works for us."

"Yes, Mr Ryan."

"And, Barnes?"

"Yes, Mr Ryan?"

"Don't take any crap from anyone, understand?"

Barnes' mouth twitches fractionally, despite the dour face. "Perfectly."

Cliff nods appreciatively. "I'll be in my office."

In between dealing with issues and situations that serve to illustrate how new he is to the job and how good Barnes is at his, Cliff spends a great deal of time studying back copies of The Globe, discerning his editors and reporters. While decidedly enlightening, he can't say he's all that surprised; if he wasn't feeling so upbeat he could find himself overwhelmed by a sense of defeat. Onward and upward, isn't that what they say?

Barnes returns to him with a schedule. "The Editors will be here at one, directly after lunch. Here is a copy of the timetable and locations for the others."

"Thanks. How did they take it?"

"I managed to remain sludge-free," he says with an air. "Will there be anything else?"

"No. Go to lunch."

"I always purchased lunch for Mr Wexford first."

"I can handle my own lunch, Barnes. Go eat. This schedule looks fine. Thanks."

He hardly notices Barnes retreat. He continues his reading and then looks up from the pile of work on his desk to find Barnes before him again.

"Didn't you leave?"

"I'm back with your lunch. A man doesn't need to be a genius to see you were going to forget to eat."

A packet of food emitting fresh, appetizing aromas is placed on his desk.

"Barnes, I think we're going to get along."

"I'm not a political man, Mr Ryan."

"Then how on earth did you manage to work here all this time?"

Again, the dour face looks like it wants to smile, but doesn't. "I'll inform you when the editors are here."

And when they do arrive, not one of them is happy to hear that their new managing editor wants to check all copy and headlines before they go to print until further notice. Their questions and protests are brutal, and their sense of self-entitlement frustrating. But they leave his office knowing the score; change is before them.

Not for one moment did he think this was going to be easy. But if nothing else, Wexford had got one thing correct: Ashcliff Ryan is his father's son. It's taken him some time to come to grips with it, but there was no use pretending that his determination and drive to get things done came out of thin air. After the Great Fire it took his father all of two weeks to have the smoldering ruin of the old Globe building cleared; two weeks after that the plans for the new building were already drawn up, and then a further week for the foundations to begin. New printing presses arrived six weeks after that. Of course it always helps to be one of the wealthiest men in Chicago. Dominick Ryan commandeered whatever he needed, purchased whatever was necessary to see the job done. He brought his money into town in the days when Chicago was mainly an abattoir; doubled it, tripled it... did with it what he willed. Success was his religion. After the fire had devastated the city, he published The Globe from a temporary shed in the grounds of their Prairie Avenue home. Later, the Mayor awarded him for bolstering civic morale during the reconstruction, which, as far as Cliff is concerned, was his father's only laudable achievement with The Globe.

Phillip calls by late in the day. And it's been a long one.

"I've come to take you home before you do more damage."

"I've only just begun."

"That's what worries me. Take a look at this."

Phillip tosses a rival newspaper onto Cliff's desk.

A bold headline flashes across his vision and sticks his gaze.

DOMINIC RYAN'S HEIR RETURNS, SET TO TURN GLOBE ON ITS HEAD

"Huh! That didn't take long," he says, picking it up.

> The heir to Dominick Ryan's newspaper empire, Ashcliff Ryan, has returned to Chicago, taking up the post of managing editor of The Globe and not Chairman of the Board as expected. That position remains with Phillip Ryan. Rumors abound that the rebel heir will change the ideology of The Globe and strip it of its infamous reputation...

"Sure you know what you're doing, Cliff?"

He throws down the newspaper. "I'm sure. And know this, Flip. We will never *ever* refer to this organization as an empire. We are a business. We employ people. We don't have slaves, or lackeys, or hired help. No one person is more or less important than another and anyone who doesn't like it can get out. We're also going to review conditions and wages for the men in the print shop."

"Give in to the Union? Are you crazy? You'll have every industrialist and factory owner baying for your blood! They're going to call you a bleeding heart socialist, that's what. A fine title for managing editor of The Globe."

"And one other thing, if I hear we've refused to employ any more migrants even though they have the skills we need, or employ them so we can pay squat wages..."

"All right, okay!" Phillip holds up his hands. "I get it. Loud and clear. It's a brand new day around here. Your old man is turning in his grave as we speak. But... well, I can't say I'm surprised. Next you'll be saying that The Globe will only print the truth."

Cliff grins. "Now you're getting the hang of things, Flip."

Luke

Provincetown, Cape Cod
Leaning against a lamp post in the sunshine

He's lost track of time. *Liberty Keep*, on the other hand, has run out of time as the seaside home of the Sullivan family. A *For Sale* sign swings in the salty breeze. Beneath the cloudless sky a seagull hovers above.

It's one of those situations when you don't want to look but you can't help yourself. Reckon the jury at Porterfield's trial would've felt that way looking at the photos of the basement… intrigued and revolted at the same time. There was nothing wrong with the outside of Porterfield's house either, same as this one, but the underbelly? – now that's a different story. There's this feeling going on inside of him that won't leave him alone, the kind that he's learnt the hard way never to disregard. So until he has looked this house of bizarre cruelty in the eye, for however long it takes, and gone down the harsh road of her life with her, he won't go to her.

The house stares back at him. Serene. Oblivious. *Inanimate, chucklehead.* No… deceptive.

Jennifer never understood about his need to come with her; and he didn't want to understand that this was something she needed to do by herself. But in either case, neither of them is totally alone. And never will be. Their spirits are entwined so that they will never be truly alone again.

It is a wondrous thing.

Comforting. Invigorating. Puzzling.

And as startling a revelation as he has ever had.

Time ticks over.

That sense of panic he had at Frank and Jeanne's seems like a distant memory; he's calm. It's also one of those situations where you are so overwhelmed by the need to do a certain thing it freezes you up; your mind is doing all the work, and your body won't move. He's rooted to this spot across the street from the house. No doubt when it's time to move he will; when his mind has finished with thinking.

The sign creaks loudly every so often when the wind picks up.

He has to admit he's come a long way from the moment when Jennifer divulged her upbringing and his only thought was to shoot Dermot. Now that the man has gone for good, and after all that has happened to them since then... let's say he has finally *matured* enough to know better.

It's kinda painful to know that Jennifer thinks of him as immature. He's disappointed in himself; he has to suck it up and show her he can do better, which he knows he can. She'd looked beyond all his faults into his heart and his spirit, never giving up on him, to the point of breaking her promise and believing he could rise above the disappointment and be the man she trusted.

And now she's waiting for him.

He thinks now that a kind of misery living deep inside him was holding back his rightful maturity. Keeping him a boy in many ways. Trying too hard to rise above his loss and Sara's fears; seeing humility as a weakness and, despite Mart's example, not truly understanding that strength of character is quiet. Humility is a sign of maturity and strength; he's seen it in Cam and in Cliff. And with it a kind of nobility. Go hand in hand, those two traits. K was never backward about pointing out his lack of both. He hated it when she did that; it certainly didn't help. But she was young, too, and still fathoming what it took to be happy herself.

How does anyone know how to be happy? Comes natural to some; it seems to find others. And others have to work at it. For some, their burdens are light; for many folks not so much. But since all the darkness in his life has gone, since he and Jennifer are both safe from the cruelty of the past, he should be more than capable of making himself and Jennifer sublimely happy.

He recalls that night in San Francisco when he stood on the pier watching Jennifer leave… he knew at that point he didn't have a clue how to make either of them happy, not really. He only knew that he wanted her to be because she deserved it. And he got a sense of what happiness might be like when he was with her.

They'd both come a long way since that night. Now he's on the opposite side of the country, before another ocean, contemplating similar questions but with a whole bunch of hindsight and so many more answers. He married that shining angel who came to him on the pier, and he has everything he'll ever need.

Ethan told him to be happy but he didn't tell him how. Ethan knows he's got it in him. If he and Jennifer make each other happy, then that's all there is to it. That's what Ethan meant.

Once Red Sky told him… *Luke, when you are older you will understand that life is like the great river, sometimes we are still and sometimes we flow where the current takes us.*

Jennifer expressed it another way when he asked her…

Why am I a river man?

You're restless… you have deep, still pools, but your life needs to be fluid… moving, creating and finding a way

Seems like knowing yourself and being happy go hand in hand.

You should write down your stories

I will if you ask me

He's been writing them ever since.

And that makes him happy, too; that, and sketching.

And horses.

And sketching horses.

And when so much happiness is waiting for him, why is he still staring at that old house?

A feeling stirs inside him. His booted foot slides itself down the lamp post and strikes the sidewalk.

He and the house are not done with each other.

Keep

Young man has been standing and staring for quite some time. Indeed, how would lamp post stand up without him? It is pleasant to be object of admiration, however young man has much more than white walls, pretty rooms and cupola full of ocean views on his mind. He is determined, this one.

Ah!

He moves at last.

He is coming.

He has worked it out.

Things he wants are here.

Been here for many, many years. Waiting for him.

Time has come to give them up.

Come, come, young man.

But don't think it will be easy.

Ghosts.

Memories.

Front door is unlocked for you.

Find what you seek.

Keep is ready.

Luke

"It's haunted."

Luke glances sideways towards the voice and does a double take. A person is standing next to him. A small woman. Not old, but not young either. Her sallow face has no lines, but her expression seems tired, as though there should be lines. Her eyes are dull; they could be blue but the tone is so flat he can't be sure.

"Excuse me, Ma'am?"

Her head turns toward the house. "*The Keep*. Do you believe there are such things as ghosts?"

"I… Not sure."

"You go in there, now there's no one at home, you soon will."

"I will?"

"When the family lived there, you couldn't tell. It all went quiet. But when they returned to Boston… you could hear it."

"Hear what exactly?"

"A woman. Singing to her child. But no people were at home."

"I know two people who used to live here, and they never mentioned it being haunted."

"Maybe the ghost liked them and let them be. Or maybe the ghost was scared of the owner."

"Did you know him yourself?"

Her head turns and her gaze comes back to him. "Interesting. Most people would ask how a ghost could be scared of a living person, assuming the reverse as is the custom."

"Are you a neighbor, Ma'am? Did you know him?"

"As much as anyone could know such a man. Lost his wife the

day his youngest child was born. Folks think it's her, singing to the babe but the babe weren't born in this house. Folks believe what they want to believe. Sweet little thing, she was. He was a brute. Perhaps the ghost attached itself to him and came with him here."

Attached itself? That can't be right.

"You seem to know a lot about this kinda thing."

"You hear talk, from time to time." She's obviously a sick woman; probably running a fever and plainly needs to rest. "Are you going in there?"

"If it's unlocked, otherwise..."

She's taken to staring at him.

"Er, don't you worry about me, Ma'am."

"I feel as though I have seen you before somewhere."

"Couldn't have. First time in Provincetown for me."

"I see. Pardon me then."

"So long, Ma'am. You take care of yourself."

He tips the brim of his hat, opens the gate and heads up the cobbled front path towards the door.

He expected it to be cold and dark inside, its old stone walls veined with anger as well as cement...

Instead it's warm and bright, alive with dust motes dancing up and down shafts of sunshine like doing this is their life's work.

Isn't it meant to be brooding and tortured, Jennifer's version of Porterfield's basement? What is this betrayal of his intention to loathe this house?

Maintaining a clinical eye, he moves through the ground floor, with its deeply-silled windows framing priceless vistas of the topaz sea on the other side.

A charming, empty house.

He doesn't doubt for a second the agonies Jennifer suffered within these walls, but as he stands beside a sizable hearth in what is likely the parlor, with busy dust motes surrounding him, it seems to him that Jennifer's house and this house are not one and the same.

How did that happen?

He flicks a glance through the wide archway which frames the front entrance where a staircase leads upward. He pushes his hat back and scratches his head.

That way then? Why not…

Things change half way up the stairs. The air is cooler. And although there are as many windows and doors as downstairs, with all their corresponding rooms off a long hall running the length of the house, the sunshine doesn't seem to penetrate and those frantic dust motes are nowhere to be seen.

Having found them kinda reassuring, he misses them, those little dust beasties. He peers into one room, the largest, thinking he's losing his marbles. If he's not careful he'll start to hear singing.

Training his gaze around the empty space, he spies a balcony through some French doors; oblong squares mark the old wallpaper where pictures used to hang; and… nothing. It's cold and sad. If the sunshine could sneak inside and cheer the place up a bit the atmosphere would be less melancholy.

What's up with this house?

It's supposed to be throbbing with anger and cruelty which he could readily perceive and openly rail against.

Know what she suffered.

Walk a mile in her shoes.

Be here, *now* – where she wouldn't let him be before, when it counted, when Dermot was dying.

Maybe that's it… he's too late.

This place is like a tomb where the past is housed. Come here not to discover the past and revive it for a purpose, but put flowers on its grave.

He sighs and leans back against the door jamb; looks around at the old walls, lets his gaze wander the hall where he imagines four young Sullivan children ran up and down… and he can only do that because he'd recently spent time with certain other young Sullivan children.

Coming here seemed like a good idea at the time.

He swings his gaze back into the room where he spies an old crate which he didn't see on his first sweep. Right there in the middle; it's on the small side but clearly visible.

In a house completely devoid of anything, how did he not see this?

He's not sure he has the right to take a look, or even to be curious. But something tells him this is what he came to find...

It's full of papers, the crate; lying this way and that in a heap to half-full. The topmost ones are steeped in dust, which if condition is anything to go by proves they will all be old.

There's no denying, there's a lot of dust in this house. Some of it is on the move and some is weighing down what lies beneath.

Such as the contents of this box.

He pushes his hat back a fraction and settles on his haunches, dips his fingers into the crate and carefully extracts the top paper. More just like it follow on. Household accounts. Meticulously kept by the look, yet hardly worth keeping. Even so, it seems the whole box is full of them. This is not what he came to find but he'll be damned if he gives up at this point. He wanders through them with the utmost respect for the dust which preserves them.

Wait up. Here's something different, two folded pages worn at the edges. As he unfolds them, more dust launches into the air; and while he's itching his nose, wondering in what part of the attic this treasure chest has been residing for God knows how long, a familiar name catches his eye...

Aisling Sullivan.

Huh. Jennifer's mother.

He gingerly turns the papers the right way up, discerning that the edges on one side are frayed as though they have been torn from a book. The pages are filled with neat handwriting, and after he has blown away the dust, the black ink appears vivid on the aging paper.

A word here and there leaps off the page as if to scream *Read Me Please!*

Very well. He will.

Because he knows: his drumming heartbeats tell him; the hot liquid sensation infusing his blood tells him.

This is what he came to find. Not Dermot. Not anger. Not retribution. This. Whatever this turns out to be.

*This is the final journal entry of Aisling Sullivan, recorded in Boston,
on this 26th day of January in the year of 1859, and dedicated to my
children: Joseph, Miles, Francis and Jennifer. God bless them.*

*Nurse Maureen O'Malley, a good and kind woman, takes this
dictation on my behalf. I cannot write for time is short and I am weak;
it will not be long until I leave my babies. God help them.*

*They are beside me on the bed. Frank, half-crying, sang to his baby
sister the lullaby I always sing to him, and now they are both asleep.
Like angels. Frank's arm lies like a shield over our tiny new girl, so
fresh from heaven. Sweet gentle babies, so beautiful and perfect.*

*Earlier I said to him, will you love our new baby for me? She will
need you. And he replied, I will, Mama, always; she will be a good
baby, but if she should be naughty sometimes, I will love her like you
would, Mama, I promise.*

*My extraordinary little boy. He kissed me over and over with his
little boy kisses, sobbing. I know in the depths of my soul he will not
break that promise.*

*My body is this terrible wrecked thing. My heart can no longer
sustain it. I have tried for hours to stop this from happening but it
cannot be stopped. I am failing and will be gone by morning. I will go
before they wake. It will be as if we went to sleep together. But I already
told my boys that I will not wake when they do, that even though my
body lies here, my spirit will be gone to heaven to live with the angels,
that we will see each other again but not for a long time.*

*Even as my body is this wrecked thing, my heart is more torn
apart at having to leave them. To desert my baby girl now may God
forgive me, yet in my soul I know she will be wonderful and exceptional
and kind. None of this is her fault, not ever should she be made
responsible. How could I rest in peace otherwise, or any of us be at
peace?*

*This is our fate. Hers and mine. Where birth and death meet at the
same door of life. Greet and farewell with one kiss before they pass by
until such time as they meet again.*

*My Jennifer and I cannot be truly separated, for her arrival
breathes meaning into my passing, and my departure will define her life*

forevermore. She should know me within herself, for this day is stamped on her heart just as it is stamped on my soul. Whether she knows it or not, I will be with her always, even as we tread different paths. Our entwined beginning and end is the source of all abounding and lasting love. She is dearly and most wholly loved.

How cruel to be her mother but not journey all the days of our lives side by side, and yet how wondrous this day when that wisdom greater than all wisdom designs a journey to begin and end at the same time, to split what should be one into two for His own remarkable purpose.

I will not be sidetracked by any bitterness. I believe my sorrow is too great for anything else anyway.

I have given the world a gift; and I gave Dermot a gift – a perfect daughter who can love him into a good and wonderful father beyond his wildest dreams, his shining angel amidst all the men in our family. A winsome creature who will charm them all, but most of all her father. Such is my dream for them. For even though the eternal light is beckoning me, my dreams for this life are as strong as they ever were. Soon enough I will fade – please God my dreams never will and they will come to pass.

I pray for Dermot; he will need it. Soon it will be time to fetch him for that peculiar goodbye wrought only by death. I cannot succumb to fear for the living, even as my sorrow at leaving is so great, and yet I wonder what he will become when I am gone. And fear that he will resent me for being weak. O God, please grant him the strength to raise our babies well, and he allows Michael to help him. Dearest Michael knows all my wishes. And I know, O God, you will not refuse my prayer.

And to you, my children, my fervent last wish and prayer is that you will find true and lasting happiness; and God bless those who give it to you. Your loving mama, Aisling.

P.S. Goodbye, my treasures, God bless and keep you. Love each other. Be strong and good. Be kind. Love and goodbye, until we meet again, the moment for which I already long.

Luke

Winthrop Street, Provincetown

He stops on the sidewalk near the entrance where a wide trail dissects a sea of grass and white stones. While he catches his breath after the long walk, he trains his eyes across the scene. There isn't a puff of wind, not even a sigh. All the bones are resting, all the souls at peace. He figured when he came here he would have to look death in the eye; and he's come to realize the voices of the dead are rarely silent. The hum of their stories, the whisperings of their secrets, abide behind the veneer of sacred silence and wait their chance in the spaces made by thought and memory; he is not fooled by all this calm and quiet.

Nor is he physically alone.

He can't deny it; his heart is really beginning to pound hard against his ribs. Well, she's there, isn't she? Right there! Out in the sea of grass with its white tips.

An instinctive voice in his head is screaming *run to her, now!*

Once he would have acted on it, as if the impulse was the most important thing in the world. Instead, he reins it in and observes with a tingling delight he is glad is now mature enough to enjoy.

Oh yeah, he will go, but not before he takes in the color of her dress, the way the sunlight falls across her shoulders, and the ever so small bump in her slight figure that wasn't there when he last saw her – the tiny prospect, safe and sound as promised. She looks down at a grave lately made. Dermot's? That's strange.

So, her neighbor in the cottage next to hers said this is where she'd be; she'd mentioned it as she passed, he said; he was watering his rose bushes at the time and cut her one to take to *her beloved*; she asked if he would be kind enough to give her another, which he did, and she left for the cemetery with one pink and one yellow; he was proud of his roses, so a lengthy explanation of why followed, and considering it isn't yet summer and the man's roses looked a picture and his Provincetown accent was a kind of fascination, Luke found himself listening for a spell; after all, Jennifer spent so much of her childhood here.

"...now the wild Beach Rose, she grows up and down the coast, on the dunes, wherever she likes and naught can stop her. They don't call her wild for nothing. Didn't know the lass had a husband, you'd better go locate her then."

And just like that he was dismissed from his rose lesson and on his way.

He takes a deep breath and begins his walk.

At that moment a breeze springs up, salty, yet as sweetly scented as the grass and bringing with it the smell of earth; it lingers for long enough to push at Jennifer's dress, which is a rich pink at the bottom and light colored and patterned with flowers at the top. A wide-brimmed straw hat tied beneath her chin shades her face from the spring sunshine. Her hair is drawn to the side to drape over one shoulder. He pictures that pretty face he's about to see. No wonder the man gave her roses.

The sound of his boots on the trail draws her gaze from the grave to him; he stops dead in his tracks a few yards away. The gladness inside him is like a stampede.

Her shocked expression gives way to her paintable smile.

Which wobbles.

And returns.

And wobbles again. "How did you..."

"Roses."

"Mr Crouch."

"Jennifer..." He closes the distance between them, folds his arms around her and lets the stampede pulverize their difficult parting and weeks of separation into oblivion.

"Oh, Luke, you came at last," she's murmuring.

An understatement.

He holds her close while the ferocious rip which had separated them repairs itself. Torn their hearts may have been, but no longer; in an instant they are whole again and every part of him knows it. He releases one hand to stroke her cheek. "Look at you, my sweetheart. How are you? And Evan?"

"We are perfectly fine, both of us. And you?"

"*So* perfectly fine," he grins.

She laughs gently. And he kisses her. And when he stops, the look on her face almost melts him at the knees. She didn't stop loving him for an instant; she has missed him as much as he's missed her. She's not angry or resentful or peeved. She's knee-meltingly glad.

She holds his face between her cool, gentle hands. "I would lie awake every night and listen to the waves, imagining that the next wave or the next or the one after that would be the one that would bring you here. In the morning I would walk down to the beach searching for you as if the ocean had washed you up on shore and I could take you home."

"Don't you think it was my turn to find you?"

"Definitely!" she laughs again. "But hope hardly ever takes a back seat." Her smile drifts away then. "I wish you had washed up on the beach, not wandered into this place..."

"I came through St Louis actually. Spent a night with the tribe. Frank told me what happened."

"Then you know everything there is to know."

"Mm, that's true. But you don't, Jennifer. Neither does Frank."

"I don't understand."

"You will. There's a bench over there. Let's sit while I explain."

"Very well."

He tells her what happened at the house, everything, in precise detail.

Except for one thing he's not sure she'd believe since he's having a hard time believing it himself... When he came downstairs that woman from the street was in the parlor. His heart almost jumped out of his chest. She was standing by one of the windows and staring out to sea, singing what sounded like a lullaby. 'Ma'am,' he said, 'what are you doing here?' 'Singing my little one to sleep of course.' She hushed him. 'We live here,' she said, 'and now that the evil old man is dead my little one will be safe from him and we can be here in our own home and remain in peace.' There was no kid that he could see or hear. He told her goodbye, left by the front door, closed it and never looked back. He's not sure he'll ever make sense of it. Best to leave the telling of it for another time and place. Or maybe pretend it never happened.

Instead, he brings the journal pages from out of his pocket and shows them to her.

Her face turns pale and she stammers, "This is what you found, and it's Mama's?"

"Yes."

"Truly?"

"Truly. Do you want to read it alone... or I could read it to you if you want?"

She nods. "You read it to me. I think that's best."

So he reads it, and aloud this way it feels as though Aisling has some presence among them.

When he has spoken the final word, he looks up at her. Immediately, he reaches into his pocket for his handkerchief and starts mopping her cheeks.

"I don't know what to make of it..." she keeps muttering. "I don't. What is this? I don't understand. Luke..."

He carefully folds the pages and puts them into her hand. "Here is your Mama, Jennifer. And she is somethin' all right."

That breeze comes back again. Neither of them speaks for a long time. She holds the papers in one hand and grips his hand with the other.

"What are you thinking?" he murmurs.

"Too much. Too little. I'm shocked that I'm not angry. I feel... strange. You were right. I was loved. But I had no notion of how that would have felt until now. I feel it. Her words, you reading them to me... it's as though I never missed a day of her love. How extraordinary. Poor Mama. Poor, poor thing."

"Mm."

"And Frank. His promise to her. He never... I'm... I..."

"I think he must be very like her."

"I think so, too. I...I know it wasn't my fault, but I did this to her. I need to make my peace with that, Luke. She would want me to."

He doesn't know what to say to this. Not a clue. So he nods.

With great care she inserts the papers into the pocket of her dress; then she tugs on his hand. "Come..."

Before long they are back in front of Dermot's grave and Jennifer is saying, "I had no idea she was buried here. Dermot laid her to rest in an unnamed grave. But you see, Joseph and Miles had this gravestone made, which is Dermot's of course, but it includes her, and now everyone can see where she is..."

And right there on top? Two roses. One pink, one yellow.

"Let me read to you this time..."

He follows along as she recites, her tone soft with emotion.

AISLING SULLIVAN
WIFE OF DERMOT SULLIVAN
MOTHER TO JOSEPH, MILES,
FRANCIS AND JENNIFER
DIED JANUARY 26TH 1859 AGED 28 YRS
NEVER FORGOTTEN, FOREVER LOVED
AT REST

She swallows hard before she continues, "Joseph was adamant the stone included them both, to show they are reunited. It's been done well but quickly, only put in yesterday. I sensed Joseph didn't want to come back here for a long time. He sent me a telegram asking me to inspect it and let him know if it's satisfactory. I think it looks sufficiently dignified."

"Me, too."

"I always assumed Mama was in Boston, not here. Frank told me long ago he and my brothers were never permitted to know; they weren't even permitted to attend her funeral. Dermot went away after she died, leaving us all in Boston. He was away for a very long time. It all makes perfect sense now. He brought her here, put her in an unnamed grave and mourned her. Gradually over time her whereabouts faded from people's interest. I wonder at my

Uncle Michael not saying anything. He was dealing with his own grief, I suppose. And more than likely he thought it not worth Dermot's wrath in revealing it to us, the ramifications for me in particular. What a peculiar, angry man Dermot was. I wonder what my mother loved about him…"

"Crossed my mind, too."

"I'm not surprised. And your conclusion?"

"I reckon she knew how much he needed her, and being needed is a powerful thing for some people, especially one as loving as your mama."

"Yes, I see what you mean. That's very astute. And very you."

"Whatever his redeeming quality in her eyes, we have you as a result and that's good enough for me."

"Oh, Luke, I…I have this strange feeling that's so strong… I want so very much to lay down on that ground and hug it as though I could put my arms around her somehow and thank her… I feel now that perhaps she wasn't so far away, and had I known that, known how much she loved me, it would have been easier somehow…"

Her voice breaks and sobs replace words. She was supposed to have known; Dermot was supposed to have given them the journal. Not to mention carry out Aisling's wishes. Such an asshole of a man. He shakes off that stab of anger and gets back to the job at hand.

"Jennifer, that business is all over now," he soothes her. "It's in the ground, literally. Dead and buried."

"Oh, Luke, honestly," she reproaches him as she dabs her face.

"And here you are, as wonderful and kind and exceptional as Aisling said you would be."

"What are you getting at?"

"Only that you are not nearly as damaged as you think you are. You were never a victim, you have always been a survivor, and with Frank's help you grew strong enough to bear a crushing load. I thought it was my job to do that too, but I was wrong. I get the good part; my job is to celebrate your victory with you and help you enjoy the spoils."

Took him a long time to understand it.

"The connection between you and Aisling has always been there, so hug her if you must, in your heart and your imagination, I guarantee you she'll be there hugging you back. She loved you more than anything and she gave it all to you as her parting gift, her strength, Frank's promise and her love and compassion. So now you can let go of all the pathetic nonsense Dermot made up. You have scratched and crawled your way out from under a tyranny of pointless misery and with the utmost grace and dignity walked into the light. You're like the wild beach rose that *naught can stop*. You're not defeated in any part of you. For as much as they are dead and buried, you are alive and thriving. And there are no more battles to fight, no injustice to rage against. It's all over and you won. You can heal your heart once and for all."

Her watery glance meets his and stays for a long time before it swings down to the grave at their feet. Wonderfully, he'd seen in those prairie green depths a confirmation of everything he'd just said.

Peace descends in nature's silence of breeze and birdsong. He holds her close to his side, her head on his shoulder; he hears her sigh, feeling the rise and fall of her chest; it's a deep one.

"I'm sorry, Mama, that my coming into the world took your life from you and from all of us. I'll always love you and I'll never forget you because you will always, *always* be in my heart. Be at peace. Until we meet again…"

He sighs, too, and kisses the top of her head. "Sara used to say *'all streams flow into sea, but the sea is never full. To the place where the streams come from, there they return again.'* Life is just one big circle, the sea, with hundreds of connecting pathways, the streams. Nothing really leaves or ends. Everything is connected and flows, including my tears and yours. You and I are meant to be."

He'd wept after reading Aisling's journal. Streams of tears. To the end of his days his heart will ache and grieve for the passing of a woman he never knew and yet somehow loves… the woman who gave him this shining angel who filled him with her light in his darkest hour.

"You know, Luke," she whispers after a minute or so, "you are becoming quite eloquent."

Not long after, they walk out of the cemetery and leave that place. Returning to it is unlikely for the foreseeable future.

As picturesque as Provincetown is, they depart after two days and head to Boston. Here they accomplish a lot: buy some much needed new clothes; visit the graves of Sons of Liberty legends Sam Adams and Paul Revere at the Granary; take in the stirring sights of the city where a revolution was made; and arrange a visit with Joseph and Miles – only one, and just them, no other family, on this Jennifer is strict, where the final journal entry is perfunctorily shown to them and received by them with as much warmth as a day in December, confirming what he always believed that mutual indifference is the limit of the relationship between sister and brothers.

This time is one of purposeful activity and amazing experiences punctuated by episodes of peace and passages of introspection. He should record its detail and sketch its beauty, but his instincts tell him these days are for his heart to keep account of, and it will as long as he lives. Maybe one day he will write them down, someday pencil them into another dimension. At this time such an account would most probably read as sentimental or like a travel memoir, and it should be neither; he didn't want to write either of those things. All he really knows is that these days will forever influence everything he writes, speaks, draws, acts, thinks, believes and loves, in ways he can't yet imagine. When the heart is completely healed, all the joy the world holds becomes attainable.

Time to head home.
But which route to take?
"I'm sure I came the long way," he says as they consult a map.
Jennifer laughs at him. Eventually, she suggests, "Why don't we go through the north, along the lakes? It's warm now and the scenery will be pretty. We could visit Cliff in Chicago and tell him about Evan and ask him, you know, what we agreed on…"
He had already spent a great deal of time telling her about the conclusion of the trial, about the sentencing, and about Cliff, how they nearly lost him, his citation, Easter, and their sad departure.

Once she had recovered from her dismay and shock over Cliff, she reflected, "I think he learnt so much about himself in Cheyenne. I think Emmaline saw to that, whether she intended it or not."

"I always thought he knew himself pretty well."

"Even you would agree that there is always something to learn about yourself."

"Nothing could apply to me more."

And then he told her all the things Cliff had confided in him.

"But I think you already knew…"

"He told me *some* things because I was his doctor as well as his friend, and I needed to know his next of kin. I certainly didn't know everything you have told me. What a remarkable man he is. We will see him again," she added with a confident smile. "I'd like him to be Evan's godfather. After all, if it weren't for him, Evan wouldn't even have a father. Yes?"

He kissed her and said, "Genius, my dear doctor."

And now the conversation has come full circle.

"You don't want to go back through St Louis?" he checks.

"I've never been to Chicago. Have you?"

"Ah, no, Jennifer," he says, frowning. "You've been my north, south, east and west and every other point on the compass, and Chicago hasn't come up till now."

She grins. "I'm curious to know how Cliff is doing."

"Me, too." He smiles back. He understands. In her condition her energy has limits. But also, what Cliff has been up to and exactly what goes on in Chicago have been questions rattling around in his brain and needing answers for some time.

She takes his hand and looks into his eyes, and while he's melting like snow in the sun and thoroughly enjoying the sensation, she says, "Things will be different once we have the baby."

There's excitement is that statement. Like they'd tamed the future somehow; made a path through it. "Chicago it is."

"Excellent. Luke, why do you rub your head every so often?"

"Do I? Probably that odd headache I get now and then. I feel great though. Like I could take on the world. Now don't look at me like that. I'm as fit as a fiddle and as good a specimen as you will ever find and what's more," he grins, "you know it."

Her eyes twinkle as her arms enfold him. "I know it, my blue-eyed boy, I know it."

Surprise all round when Joseph comes to the train the next day; he calls out Jennifer's name just as they are about to board.

"I won't keep you long," he says, indicating he appreciates their schedule and the activity around them. "Miles must attend court, otherwise he would be here also. He asked me to give you both his best."

Jennifer is about to respond when Joseph puts an old book into her hands, stopping her in her tracks.

"This is our mother's journal. It came to us after Frank left. Miles and I want you to have it. This is a sincere wish on our part. The last pages are torn out, the contents kept hidden from us; we believe it was our father's doing and having read the pages the other day it explains a great deal. He did not honor our mother's memory the way he should have. That is abundantly clear and something Miles and I will have to come to terms with. Now you have in your possession the torn pages. And while we do not comprehend the manner in which Luke came across them, we are very grateful to you for your generosity in allowing us to read them and know our mother's thoughts and love for us on that important day. She would want you to keep the journal with you, and Frank will want to see it also. She was a beautiful and loving mother to us, and I believe whatever goodness is in us came from her. We were a happy family once long ago. Miles and I wanted you to know that because that's what she wanted us to remember. She truly is a beacon of hope.

"And lastly I wanted to express my gladness that you have found happiness with Luke. You deserve it and always have, and I hope you will believe me, that I mean what I say. Stay in touch, Jennifer. Farewell and a pleasant journey to you both."

He clears his throat, tips his hat and walks off.

They are speechless.

Jennifer's trembling hands clutch the journal like it's a sacred artefact. Perhaps she will never learn to love these brothers, and trust may prove a challenge for some time to come, but after this gesture and that speech maybe she could allow herself to no longer regard them as Dermot's evil apprentices?

And Aisling's powerful love for them all may yet prevail.

Later, as the train leaves Boston behind, heading towards their next great adventure, Jennifer takes his hand firmly between both of hers and says entreatingly, "You know, you still haven't shown me your ranch."

He narrows his eyes on her. "Can you handle miles and miles of bad road?"

She laughs. "I believe I can. I long to see everyone. And share our news of the tiny prospect."

She longs to see them and share their news? All at once his spirit takes flight. The smile that jumps to his mouth finds its way into every layer of his being. Now they are truly going home.

...TO BE CONTINUED IN
A PLACE AMONG HEROES *Book 2*

COMING NEXT!

The Grand Saga Continues
ONE YEAR LATER...

A PLACE AMONG HEROES *Return of Hope* is Book 2 in the fifth volume of The Liberty & Property Legends saga, beginning where Book 1 *Rise of Hope* left off. Out of the remnants of the troubled past, striving to find their place in a new reality, the heroes of the Alliance must brave the journey to where they destiny is calling them. Finding the strength inside yourself to be the hero of your own life just might be the most courageous thing you've ever done.

"CHICAGO. A thriving industrial metropolis, second in size and economy to New York City, with its enormous European migrant populace, boils in a hotbed of worker discontent. Campaigns are raging for an eight-hour workday, better wages and better conditions for workers. The prognosis is for a long and bloody battle. Just as the blood of animals soaks the floor beneath the feet of abattoir workers in the Union Stockyards, will the blood of men run in the streets?" EMMALINE ROBERTS

THE GRAND SAGA OF THE WEST & GILDED AGE

THE LIBERTY & PROPERTY LEGENDS™ by Terri Sedmak

America 1880's. Lives taken, justice sought. Love won and love lost. Friendships forged and families fractured. As terror grows, heroes rise.

ೞVolume One
HEARTLAND
On the Side of Angels

Adventure and romance will not be denied anyone who has the courage to be free.

ೞVolume Two
EMPIRE FOR LIBERTY
Dangerous Lullaby

Deep in the heart of the Legends… Their darkest hour is coming.

ೞVolume Three
FIRST COUNTRY
Tinged with Rose

Unlock your heart… The grand saga of The West & Gilded Age continues.

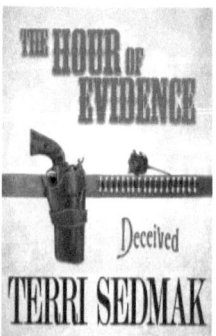

ೞVolume Four
THE HOUR OF EVIDENCE
Deceived

The scales of justice are poised… All eyes are on Cheyenne, Magic City of the Plains.

Live the adventure. Love the romance. Don't miss a moment!

The Liberty & Property Legends

Terri Sedmak

A Saga of The West & Gilded Age America

'Fast paced and riveting' - *Midwest Book Review*

'Recreations of 19th century America are evocative' - *Daily Telegraph*

'A creative, insightful and poetic writer' - *Keystone Creations*

'Compulsive reading' - *That's Life! Fast Fiction*

'Spritely and engrossing saga... ample conflict, a captivating historical context and enduring romance. Sweeping historical fiction.' - *PS News*

'One of the best fiction stories I have read.' – *Kate Matthew, Writing NSW*

'Be prepared for an insatiable need to keep on reading!' - *VANCOUVERgirl*